BIG EASY MURDERS

No Bounds

The Big Easy Murder Series Book 1

1

No bounds:
The Big Easy Murder Series, Book 1

This book is a work of fiction. The characters, and
events portrayed in this book are products of the
author's imagination and are either fictitious or are
used fictitiously. Any similarity to real person,
living or dead, is purely coincidental and not
intended by author.

An Ink and Art Original
Published in the United States by Ink and Art
Publishing   LLC, Louisiana

Cover design and Logo: Sahara Kelly, Scott
Carpenter at P and N Graphics
PandNgraphics@gmail.com
Images by RplusM photography and Sarah
Schwartz @Schwartz Photography

Ink and Art

For the only man that understands my quiet moments, all my love.

First I want to think my family for always laughing with me instead of at me. Through this roller coaster life there have been many twist turns and upside down moments. Without them the ride would not be worth taking.

I'm thankful for the many friendships old and new that make my days and nights unforgettable.

A big thank you too Sahara Kelly and Scott Carpenter at P and N graphics for all the hard-work they put into designing my covers. Many, many thanks to Sahara who keeps me from going off the rails when I lose an image and email her at midnight.

To my girl's y'all know who you all are, thanks for the shenanigans.

Chapter content:

Prologue

New Orleans, November . . .

3a.m. is a quiet time on the streets of New Orleans. Most of the bars were still open but at this time of the morning nothing much else was. Heading down the side alley of the Cathedral she slipped into Saint Anthony's Garden in the back of the cathedral facing Royal street. Elizabeth new the lock on the side entrance was not always locked. She couldn't go home yet. Others were still conducting business and she had had her fill for the night.

Slipping into the church Elizabeth made her way into the main sanctuary. Passing the altar and pulpit she headed down the aisle to the back of the church where the lights were lowest. Turning she faced the altar and crossed herself and entered the pew. Taking to her knees Elizabeth took out her rosary and started her prayers.

* * *

Sonny knelt on the bed behind his company for the night. He really enjoyed her that's why she was a regular he entertained. Running his hands over and in between her creamy smooth thighs made the head of his cock jump. He loved her soft moans and the way her arms looked stretched out tied to the hooks on the wall at the head of his bed.

Grabbing her hip's he pulled her back closer to him causing her arms to stretch tighter. Spreading her legs more he watched her sex as it glistened . . . all for him. Sliding his thumb into her she moaned tossing her head back all that silky blonde hair swept across her shoulders beckoning for his hand to fist in it. If there was one thing about Sonny Delacroix that women knew he aimed to please. Reaching up he fist his hand in her hair tightening it until her head was completely in his control. Stretching her neck back he watched as her eyes roll back as he thrust into her without mercy.

With every thrust his control threatened to slip away. With a last thrust he wrung a blinding orgasm from her and his body followed suit. He stayed deep in her sex as his body shook with the last of his climax. Sliding from her body Sonny lay down beside her as they both caught their breath. When he finally reached up and released the

binds that held her she sagged on the mattress and smiled with what could only be described as complete satisfaction.

"Give me a minute Sonny and I will go."

Sitting up he put his feet on the floor. One look over his shoulder he nodded as he got up heading for the shower. Sonny didn't invite any of the women he entertained to stay and they knew the rules. Grabbing his glass of scotch from the side table he entered the master bath. What was this his fourth glass tonight. Fucking pisser of a day he thought as he turned on the shower.

*   *   *

Here again. When would they learn, they weren't allowed, with their vile disgusting ways. Filth all of them. A stand needed to be made. Someone had to show them they had stepped over the line.

The smell of cheap perfume and sex filters around me as I make my way up the aisle. The soles of my shoes so silent she doesn't even hear me. What a pity she won't know what happened till after my hands are around her neck.

I slip into the pew right behind her leaning over my hands grab her around the neck she has no time to think no time to act. I have her in my grasp. I'm stronger then she is. I watch as I pull her back onto the pew, her eyes wide with horror. What pretty eyes, I like it when the light goes out. My body shudders from the thrill. I wish I could strangle her again for making me lust after her as she dies.

Such a shame I don't have more time to play with her. She needs to ask for forgiveness, she must finish her prayers. I walk around, slid into the pew with her. Let me help you to your knees my dear I smile into her adoring dead eyes. Brushing her hair from her face I want to place a kiss on her cheek just to mark her mine but, that won't work. No need to give the others a chance to catch me before I'm finished with my chores.

Her beads won't stay like I want them in her hands. It's okay, she can wear them wrapped around her pretty little throat.

Chapter One

*A*s the steady stream of parishioners strolled into St. Louis Cathedral, somewhere there for mass others just getting out of the cold, many were there just looking around as tourists do in a city like New Orleans. A few saw the woman on the tenth row bowed in prayer. She was in an awkward position for one kneeling so contently.

As the priest took his place up on the ……... the congregation rose for the hymnal an older woman tried sliding past the praying woman instead of going around to the end of the pew or just simply choosing another isle, she nudged the woman and to her abject horror the woman fell over. Staring up at the older woman were a pair of bulging blue eyes that held only death. The scream that rung out had everyone turning and then another scream and another as others saw what it was that had the older woman so hysterical.

Sonny sat in the leather arm chair starring at the female still sleeping in his bed, wondering how did that fucking shit happen. That fourth glass of scotch is what happened. Standing up he smoothed down his tie and slipped off his jacket. It was time for the lady to leave.

Nudging her foot, she stirred, rolling over she opened her eyes. With a wicked smile, she slipped the sheet from her body.

"Time to go d'alin".

"Already, you sure know how to shove a girl out the door."

"I haven't shoved you yet. Get dressed I need to leave."

"You could just let me stay and sleep in." she smiled.

Shaking his head, Sonny headed for the living area of his flat. He wasn't one for patience and the girls knew how he liked things. But, as simple as letting them fall asleep and wake up in his bed in the morning would make them think something had changed. Nothing had change for him. He liked things a certain way and he had no desire to change things now.

When his guest sauntered out, she grumbled a good by as she took the envelope he handed her. She knew she crossed the line on two counts. One by staying the night and two by asking to remain in his home once he left for work.

He wouldn't have her back. It was a shame, he liked the look of her tied to his bed and blindfolded. Sonny liked a certain type of woman. One with good taste and . . .a submissive nature.

Going back into his bedroom, he looked at the bed. "Damn I'm going to be late". laying his suit jacket across the armchair in the corner of the room and went to work.

Stripping the bed sheets he tossed them in the hall, grabbing another set from the linen closet he remade his bed. Once the room was squared away which meant everything put away. Sonny grabbed the sheets that had been tossed aside and headed for the laundry.

* * *

The first on the scene was a young cop, Mac hadn't been on the job that long. Stepping in to the cathedral he saw there was a shit ton of people and they were all taking pictures of the crime scene. *Son of a bitch* he mumbled. Turning around he shut the door to the sanctuary as he spotted a couple of beat cops calling them over he had them positioned at both entrances until the crime lab and homicide got there.

"Folks please take a seat with either by yourself or with those you were already with. Take the pews off to the sides please. You might as well get comfortable. No one is going to be leaving any time soon."

An audible groan came from the spectators.

When the crime lab finally arrived, Mac left the Priest he had been speaking to and directed them to the scene of the crime. Making sure the chain of evidence didn't get broken was priority. Shit like that got evidence thrown out of court. Sometimes it just happened but then sometimes it was questionable how the evidence got tainted. If the two homicide detectives he thought were going to be handling this one were who he thought, he did not want to be the one screwing up.

*　*　*

When the black Lexus rolled up a few heads turned, especially the local Leos. Sliding into an open spot, the car came to a stop on Royal street. The driver cut the engine and stepped out into the cool November morning.

"What do we have boy's? Asked Sonny as he walked across the police line.

 "The Vic is inside" one of the beat cops told him.

 "Thanks. And they're a victim not a vic."

 Stepping into the Cathedral Sonny did what all good Catholic boys did when entering the church. Dipped his fingers in the holy water and signed the cross. His mamma didn't raise a fool. Walking up the center isle he nodded to a few officers. Coming up to a fellow detective he took in the scene.

A woman around the age of twenty-five maybe thirty lay sprawled out across the kneeler between the pews. Dead blue eyes stared up at him. Black and blue ligature marks around her neck signified she had been strangled. The interesting thing was it appeared her rosary beads were wound tight around her slender neck.

The beads wouldn't have been strong enough to choke her to death. So why were they left wrapped around her neck and not left in her hands?

"Make sure we get her rosary bagged up. We will need those swabbed for DNA."

"You think this is our first rodeo, Sonny?"

"No, but it wasn't too long ago I worked a scene with you and some of the evidence was compromised. I don't like sloppy work when I'm involved."

The look the crime lab technician gave him just pissed Sonny off. Young punk would be lucky if he made it a year with the precinct. *Man, I can't wait for Jorie to get back from vacation.* "So, someone take me through what we know up to this point."

The first officer on the scene took Sonny through the events leading up to the cops being called when he was finished he pointed to an elderly woman sitting across from the priest.

"You ever know of mass being stopped due to a murder in the church?" Sonny smiled, at the baritone voice from behind him.

"When did you get back from vacation?"

"About five minutes before I got called in for this shit."

Jorie was the only person Sonny trusted to have his back. The only guy that knew his secrets and he knew Jorie's. Buddies all the way back to nappies. Jorie spent more time on Sonny's mom's sofa then his own. Jorie's father was nasty fucker who liked to hit. His old man got what was coming to him from the business end of a 45 when Jorie was fifteen.

"I was starting to think you had retired on me bitch!"

"Nah, you can't get rid of me that easy brother."

"Good to know." Sonny turned his attention back to the deceased woman. "To answer your earlier question, I don't think there has ever been a murder in this church. But, that being said we are in the city of New Orleans."

"That being said, this... Jorie pointed to the woman . . . wasn't done by a local."

"What makes you say that?"

"Sonny around here there's too much superstition for a local to come in this cathedral and lay someone low like this. Is that . . .Jorie pointed at the body . . . her rosary?" Making the sign of the cross he muttered in old French. "*Someone is about to have a bad day my friend.*"

"Well it isn't me." Sonny replied.

Sonny left Jorie talking to the officer on the scene as he went to talk with the elderly woman and the priest. Thankfully the COD had separated the two.

"Excuse me father, may I have a word with the you?"

"Detective Delacroix, yes my son."

"Father would you mind telling me what happened this morning?"

"Of course, my son, I mean Detective." The priest smiled and winked at the detective.

"Michael just tell me what you saw and stop with the my son bull. . . sorry."

Father Michaël Delacroix wasn't just Sonny's priest but his blood brother. Their mamma always said her boys were born to serve. She had got her wish, both served the community just in two separate ways.

"Tell me what happened."

"There isn't much I can tell you. I had just started mass when Mrs. Troxclair screamed. It was a chain reaction to say the least. Once the other parishioners saw what was happening they either screamed and stayed or ran for the doors. The ones who are sitting in groups over on the side are tourist mostly. A few are parishioners. I came down the aisle to see what Mrs. Troxclair was screaming about. To be honest I thought maybe a rat had gotten in. When I saw the young woman, I froze for a moment. I didn't touch the body. I led Mrs. Troxclair over to sit down away from the scene and asked everyone to take a seat while we called the police. When I got back people were taking photos like it was some kind of tourist attraction. Shameful. That's all I have for you."

"Thanks, see you at moms on Sunday."

"You will be at mass." It wasn't a question that Michaël asked but more of a statement. Sonny just saluted him with two fingers and stepped off to talk to Mrs. Troxclair'

 As Sonny approached the look of the woman he was in for a very detailed story, which meant he would have to take half of what she said and file it under bullshit and then another half filing it under doesn't add up which will leave him with about maybe a fifty-fifty chance at what really happened.

"Mrs. Troxclair, I am Detective Delacroix would you mind telling me what happened in your own words.

"Are you family of Father Delacroix's?"

"Yes, ma'am he's my brother, so can you tell me what happened."

"Oh, I don't know if I can remember everything, but for you I can try." she smiled up at him. As she explained in great detail the events as she remembered them Sonny jotted down every word so in the end he could pick through it.

"Ms. Troxclair, thank you for your statement if you wouldn't mind I will have one of the other officers come over and get some personal information from you."

"Why?"

"Just in case we need to ask you any other questions."

"Oh, okay young man."

Walking away Sonny signaled for Jorie to step over. "Anything under the body when they moved her."

"No not a thing. Everything within arm's reach appears to have been wiped clean."

Sonny just looked at Jorie and back to the pew. Well one thing for sure, if the killer had time to wipe everything down then this was premeditated. This could easily be a personal kill.

Looking around the cathedral he took in every inch of the church. Where would a killer hide? If it was personal and the victim didn't have any defensive wounds, she wasn't afraid of her attacker. If it was a crime of conveyance. The attacker could have been seen as just another parishioner. Looking at the people sitting in the side pews Sonny knew they were going to have to take every one of them down town to do separate interviews.

"Round em up take em down town to be interviewed separately."

"Looks like we will be busy."

"Welcome back." Sonny smiled.

Chapter Two

It had been a long day when Sonny stepped into the gym. He spotted Jorie working out on the heavy bag and went over. Maybe Sonny could get him in the ring. That would help him work off a bit of tension. He wasn't ready to call it a day yet, Sonny just needed a break from the paper work.

"What's that look for asked Jorie as he stopped the bag from swaying.

"What look?

""That look. Jorie pointed to the mirror. As sonny turned to look Jorie hit Sonny square in the chest. As Sonny stumbled Jorie laughed.

"Man, you're off your game or what today."

"Long night."

"But was it a good night?"

"Not getting into it with the likes of you."

"If not me than who my friend?" Jorie wiggled his eyebrows at Sonny.

"Come on let's hit the ring, you have been on vaca for two weeks let's see how soft you have gotten."

"I'm not soft asshole!"

The two men stepped into the ring and immediately drew a crowd. They always did. In their younger years both Jorie and Sonny had done some cage fighting. They still did some for benefits and charity events.

Dancing around a bit both men through some insults out. Sonny went for the body shots, Jorie always went for the take downs trying to grab Sonny around the midsection he tried in vain to slam him in to the mat. Sonny tossed him off danced back for a minute waiting for Jorie to come at him. Like a moth to a fly Jorie followed as Sonny bounced from one side to the other. When he came in for a head shot Sonny snapped out two fast jabs to his sternum.

Jorie snapped out a quick right hook catching Sonny in the side of the head.

"Didn't see that one did ya." Jorie laughed.

"Keep laughing JoJo you won't be laughing soon."

Before Jorie could counter Sonny spun around striking out with his foot catching Jorie in the side.

"Nothing to say JoJo?"

Shaking it off Jorie danced a bit smiling at Sonny. If he took his gigantic ass to the ground he would have the advantage. Sonny was better on his feet when it came to fighting, not that he didn't have game on the ground he went over the top on the ground but it took him a few minutes to get his strategy worked out that's why it would give Jorie the advantage he would be able to get Sonny's back and get him to submit smiling more Sonny really didn't like to submit.

Spinning around Jorie returned a kick to Sonny's side which in return Sonny swept Jorie's feet putting him on his ass. It would have been easy to take Jorie on the mat but it wasn't his style. He liked the stand up. "Come on JoJo get on your feet. Your holding back and why I don't know."

"You keep calling me JoJo and I will put you on the mat."

"You mean you will try", Sonny continued dancing side to side.

Jorie snapped a front kick hitting Sonny in the stomach sending him stumbling back against the ropes which Jorie saw as an invitation he lunged at Sonny hitting him in the jaw with an uppercut.

Another hit to his head Sonny stumble sideways and Jorie took him to the ground. Both men scrambled to try to take the others back as the crowd cheered on the side lines.

Jorie had just taken Sonny's back when their captain came in looking for them.

Both men got up wiping sweat from their faces.

"Rematch?"

"Not tonight, how about drinks you can by dinner JoJo."

"Sure, let's see what Captain wants."

* * *

"Father what should we do about the pew where the young woman was found?"

"Sheryl, I don't know if we can clean the area or not. I will call the detective and find out. I would hate to disturb anything. The police may have needed to come back over it."

"Very well Father. I will just be in the back if you need me."

"Sheryl where were you during all the chaos?"

"I was late today Father, happily so."

Standing their Father Delacroix watched as his aid walked away. *Poor girl*, he thought. *So alone all the time.* Glancing back at the taped off pew he just couldn't wrap his mind around someone walking in to the church and committing such a crime. Yes, crime happened all over the city even outside the doors of this very church, but never had anyone ever tarnished the inside of the cathedral like this.

He needed to call Sonny and find out how long this tape needed to stay up. Mass needed to continue schedule and having police crime tape up would both bring in parishioners that rarely came along with more tourists. Already he saw the increase of tourists all trying to get a picture of the area that was why a police man was still there. Keeping everyone at bay. *What a mess.*

* * *

Jorie walked in to the bull pit just as Sonny was hanging up the phone.

"Who was on the phone?"

"My brother, wanted to make sure they could clean the scene."

"You tell him it was good to go?"

"No I want to go over it one more time, you want to ride over there with me?"

Jorie shook his head, "Nah once was enough for me."

JoJo, I know you have always been a superstitious fuck but really, you're not going back to the scene with me.

Scratching his head Jorie just shrugged and changed the subject. "What did the boss want?"

"Don't know I was waiting on you before I talked to him, You, want to go in there with me or is that too scary for JoJo to." Sonny chided.

"Fuck you Sonny!"

"You're not my type." Sonny shook his head at his best friend. "Come on."

"Captain you wanted to see us?"

"Yes, come in."

Captain Monroe was a tall man in his late fifties. People called him the iron fist because that's how he ran his department also because he had a killer right hook. It was well known that Captain Monroe was a golden glove with the navy before entering the police department. Dark brown hair with a hint of grey at the temple along with a few fine lines at the corner of his eyes gave any indication of his age.

The men and women in the department had nothing but respect for the man. He raised his two daughters and one son all on his own. His wife Lori had been lost in a boating accident when the children were very young.

Sonny often wondered if Leslie or Les as his friends called him had ever thought about getting remarried.

"Have a seat gentlemen."

Sonny and Jorie took seats across the desk from their Captain. What transpired from that point on floored them. It seemed there had been a string of murders just like the one from that morning just in other states. The killer was never caught. The killings had stopped just as suddenly as they had started. Always young women, always with the rosary wrapped around their hands that was the only difference from the others to the new one the rosary had been wound around her neck today.

"I am having all the files brought in for you to go over. Maybe there is something that will help us with today's victim."

"How long between the murders?"

"Three years since the last one."

"Where were the others committed at?"

"All along the east coast."

"Well just let us know when they arrive and we will get right on it Captain."

Getting up both Sonny and Jorie agreed with Captain Monroe they would proceed quietly and cautiously. The feds would be here soon enough. If they could get a head start on the case and show they had established good solid leads they may be able to remain on the case.

"Sonny you know the F.B.I. is going to show up for this. If this is case turns out to be connected to an ongoing serial killer case.

We will most definitely have those assholes riding shotgun on this case."

"That Jorie is not making my day any better."

*   *   *

"Father, Detective Delacroix and Detective Michaels are here to go over the scene."

"Thank you, Sheryl," Father Delacroix watched as Sheryl wrung her hands in an agitated state. "Sheryl, is something wrong?"

"Just not feeling well sir."

"Why don't you call it a day then, See you tomorrow okay."

"Thank you, Father."

Watching his secretary, he wondered what was up with her. Sheryl was normally very orderly and very reliable. She had never been sick in the last two years she had worked for him. He didn't recall her ever being this agitated either. Today was adding up to one for the books. Leaving his office, he headed to the sanctuary to speak to the two detectives.

Entering he saw the pews had been pushed apart and Sonny was on the ground searching the under sides of them. Jorie was standing across the aisle with his arms crossed over his chest. His face was a mask of concern.

"What's he looking for Detective Michael's?"

"Who knows Father, but you know your brother as well as I do. Does he ever make since? When Sonny gets it in his head that something was missed he is on it like a blood hound."

Both Jorie and Father Michael watched as Sonny felt under the pews. When he got up he brushed his pants off looking a bit miffed.

"What's that look about brother?"

"Jorie could have gotten down there and looked for me instead of having me crawl around on the ground."

"What is the difference in which one of you gets down there?"

"He's in jeans."

"Not his fault you dress like an uptight business man."

"He is standing right here and he can hear both of you." said Jorie.

"You know my son talking about yourself in the second person is a sign that you're a little off."

"I am out, before I say something that no matter how many our fathers and hail Mary's I say will never make it right." As he walked away he called back. "The Delacroix boys are not saints."

Shaking their heads in unison they watched as Jorie left the church. Walking back to his brother's office Sonny really was a little concerned about his friend, something had been off since this morning. Maybe he could loosen Jorie's mouth over dinner and drinks tonight.

* * *

Sonny wasn't surprised that Jorie bailed on dinner. It wasn't the first time and most certainly wouldn't be the last. Sonny still wondered what was up with his partner that kept Jorie making excuses for not hanging out. There had to be a serious reason he avoided Sonny. Shrugging it off Sonny decided on grabbing dinner at The Alibi they had one of the best burgers in the French quarter.

Lucking up on a parking spot on Dauphine Street Sonny slipped the Lexus into the spot. Grabbing his jacket off the passenger seat he remembered his wallet was in the console. When he reached in to grab the wallet a picture of Jess sat on top. Sonny just sat there starring at it. He didn't carry a photo of her, ever. *Where in the fuck had that come from?*

Looking around he took in his surroundings, Sonny knew every side street, alcove, private parking area and street in the fucking city. Someone was seriously messing with the wrong man. Whoever it was would have to be someone from his youth.

Screw this shit. You want to watch me, well fucking watch me mother fucker!!!

Sonny opened the door checked his gun and shrugged on his jacket shoving his wallet into his back pocket he closed the car door and headed towards Iberville street. He never looked around one time. Sonny wasn't going to try not to give it another thought.

When Sonny stepped into the bar the feeling of being watched hit him hard. Taking a seat at the bar, he was on full alert. He counted on his instincts and they were screaming at him right then. *Mother fuckers!!*

* * *

Fresh air hits my face when I walk out the bar. It feels good to be out on the street. Sitting there watching him he didn't even notice me. The great Sonny Delacroix, didn't recognize me.

HE will notice me, he will crave me.

I see into him. I know what he wants. I know what he likes, he will see me, he will beg me by the time I'm finished with him.

Chapter Three

Driving through the dark streets of the city the murder at the church weighed heavy on his mind. What type of nut job killed a woman in a church while she prayed. There was a place in hell for him.

What did he know so far? The victim didn't have any defensive wounds on her hands, so she either knew her attacker or she was taken completely off guard. How could someone get that close without being heard? It was a church after all. How had she gotten in the church the front doors should have been locked at that time.

Sonny reached for his phone.

* * *

Jorie was sure that was the phone ringing but with Raiann's mouth wrapped around his cock he wasn't completely sure if it was just his head ringing from the sheer pleasure he was experiencing.

"Raya, baby stop for a minute."

"Really, Jorie."

"Sorry, I am on call."

Raya rolled away as Jorie grabbed his phone. When she went to get out the bed he grabbed her pulling her back down.

"Hello."

"Jorie, was the front doors locked at the time of death?"

Putting his finger to his mouth showing Raya to be quiet. "Sonny?"

"Yes, it's Sonny, do you know if the front doors were locked?"

"Don't know. Why?"

"Just thinking."

"You out driving?"

"Yes."

"You need me to ride?"

"No, I think I can drive around by myself Jorie."

"Okay anything else, Sonny?"

Jorie found himself listening to the sound of silence. Shaking hi head he hung up and laid the phone aside.

"Now, where were we?"

"Is Sonny alright?"

"It's Sonny Ray, he hasn't been alright in twenty years."

* * *

Sonny hung up with Jorie. Sonny new when Jorie had company. Jorie always answered on the second ring. Sonny caught himself smiling at that little fact. He wished he knew who was on the other end of the line that had Jorie jumping through hoops. The sad part was Sonny had always hoped Jorie would get his head out his ass and stop toying with Raya.

Being the baby sister to the Delacroix brothers made it hard for her to meet anyone. She also loved Jorie, had always loved the man. He was just foolish, chasing tail that would never amount to nothing.

Sonny dialed the only other person that could answer his question. He just didn't want to talk to Michael.

* * *

I need another, I can feel the last one's neck in my hands. Her pulse beating against my palms. Blue eyes caressed me, saw me, smiled at me. I need another, to make me feel that again.

The feeling always leaves me to soon, it never last always abandons me. Leaves me cold. I can still hear her heels clicking on the tiles. CLICK, CLICK, CLICK. The creak of the wood when her knees found their spot. Makes me ache to be there again. The smell of her hair as I leaned over her. I can't reach what I need as my own hands run over my body I want them to be hers always hers.

I left something behind, I always leave something behind. They never find it never, never.

Patience I must be patient.

* * *

"Morning Sunshine."

Sonny turned from the coffee bar in the station house break room only to have Jorie smiling at him like the cat that at the canary. He really hated chipper morning people and Jorie had always been one.

"Jorie." Sonny grumbled.

"I can see by your demeanor you haven't had enough coffee this morning."

"I'm good. Where are we on finding out who the victim was at the church?"

Jorie walked over to his desk with Sonny breathing down his neck. This was probably not the best time to tell Sonny that he was dating Raya. Sonny had seemed to take it in stride that Jorie had always liked her but, dating his baby sister would probably be a whole different matter. Deciding against the telling him Jorie picked up the file on their victim from the church.

"Victim is one Elizabeth Jones, 28. Lives with three other women in the garden district. She was in nursing school she also was doing her intern ship at children s hospital. According to her room mated she didn't drink, smoke or take drugs of any kind. She's a vegetarian and is allergic to cats. Also, she didn't hang out in bars and only worked as an escort on the weekends. She has high end clients that she attends parties and charity functions. The rest of her room mates are bartenders/escorts."

"The garden district is the opposite direction." Sonny spoke mostly to his self.

"Why was she walking if her clients are high end why wouldn't a car service have dropped her off at her home," Which was more than ten blocks away. Sonny looked up at Jorie for an answer.

"Roommates said she should have had a card that would have who when and where on it."

"We need to take a look at her personal affects Jorie."

"Already ahead of you Sonny." Sonny starred at the white board in front of him. All they had so far was a picture of the victim. He and Jorie had been over the crime scene twice and nothing had been left behind. It seemed the killer was a careful killer.

What was the deal with the rosary wrapped around her neck? Did the killer have something against the woman? There were a dozen questions.

"Sonny, what are you thinking?" asked Jorie. Sonny had been looking at the board for half hour in dead silence. Jorie needed to know where his head was at on this case.

Sonny didn't look at Jorie when he answered." I'm just wondering why the church and why the rosary wrapped around her neck."

Jorie stepped up next to his partner, "Maybe the killer simply followed her into the church and the rosary were wrapped around her neck as somewhere to pace them as simple as those answers are perhaps that's the answers."

"You know the pro-filers say that the bigger the monster, the bigger the need."

"Jorie since when do you listen to the pro-filers?"

"I'm just repeating what I have heard."

"Okay, what do we know about the crime, not the victim?"

"Let's see. We know it was a personal kill."

"Why?"

"Why what Sonny?"

"Why is it personal?"

"Come on Sonny a strangling. Its personal. Very up close and personal."

"Jorie, cruelty and violence are very human traits. As human's we only have four biological needs. Feed, fight, flee, and fornicate and they are all linked to pain and pleasure. A killer this bold want's attention. All the attention they can get."

"Why do you think that?"

"Its simple Jorie, the kill was in a very public place. The killer knew the victim would be found quickly which probably heightened the thrill. We need to analyze the first victim. We need to go over the files from the FBI. Find out if this is the same killer."

"Let's go over the files and then we can go from there."

It sounded good to Jorie. As long as he didn't have to go back to the church he would be fine. He would read every damn file twice. The murder had given him the creeps. Sure, he had seen a lot of messed up things but, just the fact that it had been in the cathedral. He shivered thinking about it. Yes, there was a special kind of hell for this individual.

Chapter Four

Looking through Elizabeth Jones belongings led them to A business man on the north shore and he had no clue why Elizabeth was not dropped off at her home. The business man gave them the number to the driver from that night.

The morning had been long. Sonny had a lunch date with his brother and signaled to Jorie he would be back after while

Walking to his car Sonny couldn't believe how the temperature had dropped in the last few hours. Reaching his car, he noticed a flier stuck under his wiper. He really despised those things. Most of the time they wound up littering the ground.

"I hate these things." snatching the paper from the wind shield Sonny unlocked the car and slid in crumpling the paper. Taking a minute to let the car warm up he looked at the crumpled paper in his hand. At second glance, it didn't appear to be a flier after all.

Smoothing out the paper he read the large block letters twice before the words sunk in.

I"M WATCHING YOU, ALWAYS WATCHING YOU.

YOU PROMISED!!

Looking around Sonny saw no one or nothing that appeared out of place. Turning off the car he stepped back out into the wind. He took a minute to look around and then marched his way back into the station house. He would have forensic take a look at the paper may be there would be DNA on it and then the asshole who left it would get a visit.

But Sonny kept re-reading the note. It nagged at him. Sonny never made promises. The last one he made still haunted him. As Sonny thought about the promise he quickened his pace. The note reminded him of more than the promise but the girl he made it too. Then he caught the scent of perfume that came from the paper. That had to be more than a coincidence.

Jorie stepped out of Sonny's way. "Sonny what's wrong?"

Sonny didn't say anything he just signaled for Jorie to follow him as he re-entered the station heading to forensics' with Jorie hot on his heels. When they entered the department, Sonny talked to the lead tech and asked them to try to remove any DNA from the paper. It would take some time. Sonny and Jorie left to have dinner and wait.

* * *

Sonny and Jorie stepped out of the NOPD. The cold November wind whipped down Royal street catching them off guard. As a chill ran through Jorie he had a bad feeling things were about to get crazier than usual.

Jorie followed as Sonny headed for his car. Trying to keep any comments to himself. Jorie knew one wrong word and he would be left standing right there on Royal. Sonny was touchy when it came to all things Jess and unfortunately Sonny's mind was stuck on a merry go round now.

What Jorie wanted to know was who knew about Sonny and Jess, enough that they could play these kinds of games with him. Slipping into the passenger seat of the car he closed the door and sat quietly. If a conversation started up it would be Sonny that started it.

Turning off Royal street onto Poydras Street Sonny finally spoke." You good with Dragos?"

Jorie nodded. Char-grilled oysters sounded good alongside a cold beer. Sonny remained quiet the rest of the drive over to Dragos his mind went back to a time and place when Jess was still with him. Jess was the love of Sonny's life what he wouldn't do to turn back the hands of time and change her fate. It wouldn't matter if his fate changed just hers so she could have had a chance at a life. A chance for a husband and kids.

Sonny could still see her dancing around his family's home. She had a laugh that was maddening was the only way to describe it. It drew you in like she held a mystery all her own. Her hair was long black and wavy the way it swayed across her back barely touching her ass begged for him to tighten his hands in it and force her to bend to his will.

When her eyes became dazed and her voice became breathy those moments made him ache. There wasn't any other way to distribute it. His thoughts brought other memories. Memories that went of sweet moments nor hot sexy ones. They were the moments that Jess became uncontrollably. Violent at times to the point she had been institutionalize on more than one occasion. Sonny loved her no matter what she did or how she behaved.

It all came crashing down around him when Jess had started demanding they go to sex clubs. Sonny had borderline on the BDSM scene but, Jess had wanted to be all the way in the life. He had refused one to many times sending her off the deep end. The result had been her ending their relationship via a dear John letter.

Sonny hadn't had time to even get in touch with Jess before he received the news she had been killed in a car accident. Sonny barely remembered the funeral. It had been a sweltering day in August the humidity made it hard to breath that day. He remembered all his family had been there. Even his brother Francis who seemed more somber then normal. Thinking about Francis Sonny realized that had been one of the last times he had seen him also.

Sonny still couldn't forgive himself for not trying harder to find a way to make things work for Jess. Part of it was guilt that he felt relieved that they were done when he read the letter. Every time he came home it was good for a day may be two at most and then all hell broke loose.

He still remembered boxing up their apartment. He had found numbers on napkins with names of men. Club passes for sex clubs that Jess had wanted to go to. It had crushed him to think what she had been doing. It also made him wonder often where had she been going that night so late. Sonny knew the answer he just didn't want to admit it. Sonny truly believed if he would have said yes and just been what she wanted Jess would still be in the world. Maybe not with him but possibly happy with someone else and still above ground.

Rubbing a hand over his face Sonny realized he was at the parking garage. Pulling in he found a spot, parked and quickly got out. He needed a fucking drink.

* * *

"What's going on Sonny?" Jorie asked as they took seats at the bar. He wanted to know where his friends head was at. There was more to the story then just a note being left on his car windshield.

Sonny said nothing as he ordered Scotch neat. Jorie order his usual a beer. He waited but Sonny said nothing until after he tossed back his first scotch and signaled for another.

"Last night…" Sonny began to tell Jorie about how he had the feeling of being watched. The feeling had remained for over an hour and then it just disappeared. Sonny hadn't noticed any one out of place or particularly interested in him. So, after dinner he went for a drive to think about the case like he often did.

"And today?" Jorie prodded.

"That note. On my car. That was something Jess would say to me a lot. I mean every fucking time we fought. Those were her exact words. The paper smelled like her."

"No Sonny it smelled like the perfume she wore. Do you know how many women probably wear that perfume Sonny? Do you?"

"Jorie, Jess wore Red2 and it was discontinued sometime back."

That brought Jorie up short. He didn't have a retort. Maybe Jorie could talk to him about Jess without it blowing up in his face

"Sonny it's not your fault what happened to Jess."

"If not mine, then who's Jorie. Tell me who's fault, is it?"

"NOT YOURS!" Jorie yelled at him. Damn it he was so tired of Sonny carrying the burden of Jess. Sonny wasn't even in the country when the accident happened. Jess had been in trouble for some time before she mailed Sonny the dear John letter breaking things off.

What Sonny didn't know or Jorie hoped he didn't know was what she had been doing while he was gone. How many times had she called crying for Jorie to pick her up from some club. Jess ventured into clubs that back then Jorie hadn't known existed. Jess laughed at him the first time Jorie had picked her up. She stank of cigarettes, booze and sex. When he asked her about the sex she had reached over the cars console rubbing her hand own his crotch. When he removed it she laughed. He still remembered that night.

Jess had gone to great lengths telling him how she liked multiple partners and she liked it rough. Jorie had told her to stop talking. That's when she started telling him how Sonny wasn't man enough to satisfy her, that he was weak. Jorie had pulled to the side of the road slamming the car in park. He remembered grabbing Jess by her jaw squeezing her so hard she couldn't speak. Jorie told her to shut up, to just shut up about Sonny. When she laughed, he shoved her back into her seat. See Jorie that's what I like she had told him. Jorie had slapped her hard across the face something he had never done in his life.

The instant he slapped her all hell broke loose in the car. Jess went nuts on him. Jorie tried keeping her off him as she slapped at him and screamed. Even began ripping at his hair. Then how it happened he still didn't know she was there straddling him begging him to fuck her. Grinding against him. His body reacted to her but not his mind. Jorie tossed her across the console pointing a finger at her she laughed hysterically and then pouted like a child,

Don't you ever fucking come on to me again Jess he had told her. Why Jorie you worried you won't say no next time had been her response.

Hey where you at over there? Sonny asked looking at Jorie.

Jorie came aware of his surroundings. *Fucking bitch!*

"Sonny, all I'm saying is, that Jess had a lot of problems. More than you probably even know about. You weren't here when she went so far off the rails, none of us could help her."

Sonny held up his hand stopping Jorie. Looking at his oldest friend he asked the one question he never wanted to know the answer too. "Did you sleep with her?"

"No."

"Did you fuck her?" Sonny asked again.

"Fuck you Sonny! No, and it wasn't because she didn't try. Now are you fucking happy? Anything else you want to know while we are having this fucking conversation about your personal demon?"

Slamming his glass down on the bar Sonny walked out, leaving Jorie starring after him.

"What was that about?" asked the bartender.

Jorie just shook his head there was no easy answer to that question. Looking back at the bartender he ordered another beer, Either Sonny would cool off and come back or he wouldn't. Jorie wished he could crawl into Sonny's head sometime and see what made him think the things he did.

Jorie knew one thing for certain, Sonny would dwell on the fact that Jess had tried to sleep with him. He just hoped Sonny could get past it. That was the real reason Jorie never talked about Jess with him. There were to many things unsaid. Looking back at the bar Jorie picked up his beer…*So much for dinner.*

* * *

Sonny paid the security guard to let him into the cemetery. The gates were closed by 4pm every day and not opened on holidays.

He didn't need the sun to be up as he walked through the rows of mausoleums. Sonny knew exactly where he was going. Coming to the end or the last row stood a dark granite tomb with one name across it... BATISTE . . . Dropping his head he spoke softly, like a whisper on the wind.

Jess, I dreamt about you again. I was walking down royal and there you were with the maddening laugh and your black hair blowing in the breeze. You stepped into that alley I tried to follow but couldn't get there this time. I so wanted to be back there again, with you.

I still don't know why it happened to you and not me, it should have been me. What were you doing by yourself that late at night, on the old highway? I have so many questions that will never be answered.

I should have protected you better. I should have moved you with me. I am sorry I failed you. I have kept my promise. You will be the only one. The only one I will ever love.

Sonny slid down the front of the tomb and just sat there leaning his head against the cool granite. There were days he didn't think about her and that left him with so much quilt. Then there were days he couldn't think of anything else. Twenty years had passed. Sonny had never looked for love again. He didn't want to feel helpless when it all went to shit.

Jess had been everything he had ever wanted and when she got sick he just didn't know what to do or how to help her. She had been diagnosed as having traits both of a sociopath and Psychopath. Sonny had refused to believe any of it. He told himself over and over she was just having mood swings. But as things went on they got worse. Jess had always been sweet and caring. She became cynical and mean. Even brutal at times.

This wasn't helping him, Sonny needed to get out of here. As Sonny stood up the wind picked up and with it a faint smell of perfume.

"Jess?"

The sound of crunching leaves had Sonny turning with his gun out and ready. It was only George the guard.

With his hands held out to his side George hadn't meant to startle Sonny. He had called to him several times but Sonny seemed to not hear him.

"Hey Sonny it's about shift change."

When Sonny didn't respond George the night security officer called to him again. "Hey you okay?"

"Yes, thanks George I'm good. Let's go. You didn't happen to let anyone else in tonight?"

"No way, my job is on the line enough letting you in as often as I do. *Which is every other night.* He thought.

"Well if there's ever anything you need you just let me know."

George looked back at the tomb. "Sonny who's in there that meant so much to you?"

Looking back over his shoulder Sonny sighed. "My heart."

George didn't say another word as they headed to the front gate. What was he supposed to say . . . that sucks or I'm sorry. It didn't seem to hold any meaning.

* * *

Sonny didn't show back at the bar Jorie knew because he waited. It seemed Sonny needed more time to cool off. Sitting at his desk Jorie wondered if Sonny would even bother coming in to the station house. They had leads to follow up with. Grabbing his gun and badge from his top desk drawer he decided he was just wasting time waiting.

Jorie didn't just run into Sonny as he walked out the station house he ran into him as almost knocking him over.

"Watch out""

Sonny...Jorie just stopped talking. Sonny was not over the argument from the night before and by the look on his face he wouldn't be for some time.

"I don't want to talk about anything but the case. You got it?"

"Sure."

"I was just heading out to follow a lead. One of our victim's roommates called said there was a and I quote "creepy guy hanging around since Elizabeth was killed." I'm heading over there to get a description and canvas the area. " Jorie walked away leaving Sonny standing on the steps of the precinct. Looking back, he called to Sonny" you coming?"

Taking a breath Sonny tried centering himself. It was going to be a long day if he and Jorie didn't hash out the conversation from last night. Walking back towards the street he motioned for his brother to ride with him. If he was driving Sonny was less likely to punch Jorie.

I don't know why we have to take your ride all the time Sonny."

" Because I prefer to drive, that's why."

Sonny and Jorie had talked to Elizabeth's roommates. Trying to get more of an idea of her day to day routine. Sonny and Jorie were still trying to find the driver from the night of the killing but it seemed he had taken a sudden vacation.

Now with the sighting of the mysterious creepy guy the girls had called about, Sonny was thinking this may have been a stalker situation. They needed to find the driver. As they walked back to the car Sonny spotted a suspicious guy fitting the description of creepy guy. Sonny whistled grabbing the guy's attention Sonny thought at first he would run but when Sonny waved him over he did just the opposite he walked over to where he and Jorie stood.

"You need something officer?

"You been hanging around here the last few days?"

"Yes. It's not a crime."

"No, it's not, but someone called about you, saying you were acting suspicious. you have ID on you?"

"Yea."

Sonny snapped his fingers letting the perp know he wanted to see it. And that's when the perp took off. Jorie took off on foot as Sonny jumped into the car. At the intersection of Prytania street and Jackson avenue the chase came to a screeching halt as the perp tried crossing the intersection causing a three-car pileup and he managed to only get clipped by the bumper of the first car.

Sonny cuffed him and put his ass on the curb while Jorie called the accident in. They both checked the passengers in the cars. One woman had minor scratches from the airbag, an elderly gentleman needed to be taken to the hospital his car had been the one in the middle of the pile up. The third SUV had a woman that seemed familiar to Sonny but he couldn't place her.

"Miss, are you okay?" Sonny was curious about the woman, there was something about her but, Sonny just could not place her. She was easy on the eyes he thought. He noticed her light brown hair and thought it may be a wig, that peeked his interest. Sonny noticed she had contacts on changing her eyes to brown. This was someone trying to hide in plain sight. His years of being a detective had him more than curious. Was this someone in trouble or causing trouble? "Do you have your licenses on you?"

"Yes, officer." The woman handed Sonny her I.D. and leaned back in her seat. "How bad is my vehicle?"

Sonny looked up from the woman's information he held in his hand. "I think you will need to go to the ER to get checked out. And your SUV is not drive-able. Mrs. Hammonds. Sonny asked just to see if she would acknowledge the name.

"Hmmm." was all she said.

Sonny suggested again she go to the hospital to get checked out. She had some apparent injuries that needed to be looked after. The woman Lori Hammonds according to her ID had Sonny on high alert. Something was going on with the woman. Sonny turned away as the ambulance left the scene. He needed to see what Jorie had found out from the perp.

Unfortunately, Jorie hadn't gotten a word out of the suspect. Which meant they were taking him downtown for interrogation.

* * *

Lori Hammonds, lay in the back of the ambulance on an uncomfortable gurney. Her mind running wild as she thought about Detective Delacroix. He was trying to connect the dots. Lori laughed silently at his feeble attempt to figure it out. She knew it she would stay with him all day. That's exactly what she wanted. Yes, the wreck was unfortunate but, it helped Lori with her plans. Fate sometimes was on your side. When she headed out this morning she had been thinking about where and how she could get next to the detective again.

He didn't recognize her once again. Lori knew she had become quite the chameleon over the years. Now she had to get herself out of the situation she was in and that being said she needed to make a call.

Chapter Five

New Orleans was known for its random and unpredictable weather so rain in the middle of the day shouldn't bother a local like him but Sonny hated being rained on.

What was that saying he thought *Don't like our weather stay longer than five minutes and it will change* and just like that the rain stopped and the sun peeked through the grey clouds. *Maybe someone up there likes me after all.*

Sonny made his way along the semi crowded streets. Jorie had asked him to meet him to watch the game and to have drinks. Something was off with Jorie, But. what it was Sonny had no clue. That's why he canceled his plans for the evening so he could talk or listen to Jorie.

Sonny found Jorie right where he said he would be at Coops down on Decatur street, a local hangout, was Jorie's usual place. As Sonny took a seat Jorie looked at him and smiled.

"Look at you Delacroix."

"What?" asked Sonny.

"You in jeans."

Shaking his head Sonny ordered a beer. Looking up at the T.V. "How's the game?" When he didn't get an answer, he looked back at Jorie, who was staring at him with a wide eye expression.

"What now?"

"Beer, you ordered a beer."

"Shut the fuck up and watch the game."

Sonny sat at the bar watching a ballgame he had no interested in. At the end of the bar sat a blonde trying to get his attention also something he wasn't interested in. What he was interested in was Jorie getting to the point. After all, it was Jory who had called and asked Sony to meet him.

Signaling the bartender Jorie ordered another beer and joined Sonny in watching the game. How does a guy tell his best friend his sleeping with his little sister?

Hell, Raiann was twenty-eight now. How mad would Sonny be? At least Jorie had waited till she was out of college before he decided to ask her out. Jorie knew what the problem would be for Sonny. The problem was no one would ever be good enough for Raya. Michael knew about the relationship and was okay with it for the most part. His only concern was Jorie being a cop. Their father was a cop and played both sides of the razors edge. In the end, it had cost his family dearly.

"What's going on Jorie?"

Jory signaled to the bartender again trying to get a beer. "What da ya mean."

Shaking his head at his brother. "I do not know, you called this meeting, Jorie."

"Just thought we could hang out that's all, Damn Sonny don't you ever just relax?"

"Bullshit !!!"

Before Jorie could respond the blonde from the end of the bar slid up to Sonny running her hand along his hard thigh. Jorie turned his head holding back a laugh. Sonny looked at Jorie and back at the woman.

"Can I help you?"

It wasn't so much a question but a statement which said get your hand off my leg.

"You looked like you could use a little company."

She wore to much lipstick and the false lashes were a bit over kill Sonny thought as he looked at her. "Not interested miss" and removed her hand from his thigh.

"Sonny you seen Raiann lately?"

Sonny looked over at Jorie and glared. He knew Jorie was in love with Raiann but had never made a move. It was a sore subject with him. Jorie would be the only guy he would trust to take care of his sister. But, Jorie only teased Raiann when she was around. It really pissed Sonny off. One of these days he would have to tell Jorie to back off or get with the program. Sonny didn't want to have that conversation. Especially because it would probably cause a rift between them. Jorie and Sonny were like a disease and its cure they walked hand in hand you never heard one's name without the others being mentioned in the same breath.

Once again Sonny was interrupted when he looked back once more at the blonde she was sliding her hand along his arm.

Cocking an eyebrow at her he slammed his badge on the bar." I told you no, I won't tell you again."

"Fine !!"

Sonny watched as she left the bar. Finally, he turned his attention back to Jory. Where were we.

"Dude you need to relax the lady was just trying to pick you up."

"She's not my style."

"What style is that, "Jory laughed. "She was female."

Sonny was tired of Jorie hem-hawing around whatever he wanted to say. "What were you asking me?"

"Raiann, have you seen her recently?"

Sonny watched the game he never looked at Jorie when he answered him. "She just got back to town according to Michael. Why are you asking?"

"Just making conversation."

Sonny didn't respond if Jorie had anything else to add he would. If Michael knew she was back in town so did Jorie. The two of them were thick as thieves. It was their older brother no one had heard from in over three years he was living somewhere on the east coast the last Sonny had heard. Francis had chosen another kind of family over their blood family. It was a bone of Contention between them.

"Michael didn't mention it to you where she had been?"

"I didn't ask him. Been busy the same as you."

"So why don't you tell me what's going on with you?"

Jorie continued watching the game. He was not normally a coward but when it came to coming between the love his life and her big brother whom Jorie would also take a bullet for he was a chicken shit mother fucker all day long.

"Nothing's going on Sonny. Why are you asking?"

"You seemed off at the church and at the gym later. Just wondering if things are okay. And where did you go on this vacation of yours? You never said where or with who you were going. Seems strange for someone who claims to tell me everything." Sonny smiled at Jorie as he turned back to the game.

Jorie glanced around the bar, It was crowded tonight due to the game being on. Fuck it he thought. Raiann deserved a man that could stand up to the devil himself if need be. Taking a long pull on the bottle in his hand Jorie readied himself for a fight.

"I was on vacation with Raya"

Sonny didn't look at him he just starred at the T.V. finally he turned on his bar stool. "What was that?"

"You heard me and I don't like repeating myself."

"It's about time, asshole."

Jorie just sat there. He should have known he couldn't get anything past Sonny.

"Sonny . . ."

"I know Jorie. Can we now watch this game so we can both get on with our evening?"

"So, we're good Sonny?"

Sonny just kept watching the game.

Nodding his head Jorie watched the game as Sonny had suggested and took a deep breath of relief.

* * *

Leaving the bar Sonny listened to Jorie ramble on about he and Raya's vacation. Sonny was starting to think he was better off in the dark about their relationship. Stopping

Sonny looked up and down the street. Everything was quiet just a few people were out in the cols November weather.

The hair on the back of his neck had that tingling sensation. Sonny felt like he was being watched again and after the fucking note he was on high alert.

"Problem Sonny?"

"No, everything is fine Jorie. What else happened on your vacation?"

Jorie laughed loudly as he slapped Sonny on the back. 'You weren't listening to me the first time around. I am sure you won't listen the second time either."

The two men walked silently down the street. Both were well aware they had eyes on them. Jorie and Sonny had been partners for years and friends longer. The two men walked back up to the precinct on Royal street the whole time they stayed quiet.

Stepping in to the station Sonny and Jorie stopped and took positions where they could see outside undetected.

"You see anyone, Sonny?"

"Nope. I know someone was watching me or us."

"I knew something was up. How do you want to handle this?"

"We keep vigil Jorie, we keep our guard up. Whoever this is, they will slip up and we'll grab em."

Sonny and Jorie had been down this road before. When you walked on the edge of things like they had done for a lot of years you knew when you were being targeted. But, what they were being targeted for this go around was something they wanted to know and by who.

"I'm not hiding in here that's for certain. You heading home Jorie."

Jorie nodded his head and followed Sonny out the station and towards their cars. The feeling of being watched stayed with them.

Chapter Six

Sonny had been looking over the witness statements from the cathedral. James king was one he had been reluctant to talk to them during his interview. The man was a salesman. Sonny wanted to take a better look at him.

Margret Helms was another that seemed reluctant to talk to them. She was in town from Maine with her husband. The husband Ralph had not been in the cathedral when the police officers arrived. Margaret did not know where he had gone off too. Sonny wanted to have both brought in for questioning. Their plans had been to be in New Orleans for another two weeks on business. They would have them brought in for further questioning.

Sunday dinner was coming and Sonny wasn't sure he even wanted to go. Sitting back in his chair he picked up the phone. Sonny wondered if his mother was aware of the relationship between Raiann and Jorie.

"Hello."

Closing his eyes as he listened to his sister's voice come over the line, this would either be an easy call or a hard one but, it was up to him how it went.

"Ray, it's Sonny.

"Hey big brother I have been waiting on your call.

That was all it took to ease Sonny's mood. "Yea, whys that," he laughed into the phone.

"Oh, I think you know why."

Sonny could hear the teasing in Raya's voice. "So, I hear you are dating a complete loser?" He laughed again.

"I have lost all sense of responsibility because of that looser Sonny but, hell I love him with everything in me."

Sonny knew that was the honest to god truth. "I'm happy for you Raya. But, if that asshole hurts you. I will kill him slowly and bury him deep."

"Sonny!! That's Jorie your talking about."

"Exactly, He laughed whole heartedly.

Jorie watched from the back of the squad room. The only person that ever brought a smile to Sonny was his baby sister. Thank god Sonny was laughing. Raya was highly protected by all the Delacroix's.

He watched as Sonny hung the phone up. Walking up to his desk Jorie was about to take a seat when Sonny looked at him. "Don't fuck up Jorie."

Shaking his head Jorie told Sonny he would not be fucking up. It appeared that after chasing down the perp on Prytania street Sonny had something on his mind. He was thinking extremely hard thought Jorie. He half expected smoke to start coming out of Sonny's ears at any moment.

Jorie cleared his throat bringing Sonny back around to the now. "You good over there Sonny?"

"Yes, I was just thinking we should go back over the crime scene photos."

"What are we looking for exactly?" Jorie inquired as he got up to follow Sonny who was already on the move.

"A killer, one that loves the attention like this one does can usually be found watching the scene unfold. They crave more. He would have been there. We missed something Jorie." Definitely missed something. Sonny continued walking till he was in front of the photo board. Leaning back against an empty desk Sonny rolled his sleeves up and crossed his arms against his chest. They had missed something. As he looked over the photos hanging in front of him, Sonny realized who they had not talked to. "Jorie, we need to bring James King back in. He did not want to be interviewed. Let's drag him back in for another interview."

Jorie grabbed his jacket as Sonny grabbed his own. Grab that folder Jorie and let's go pick Mr. King up. And Mr. And Mrs. Helms. Her husband had left the scene before police arrived.

As they walked out Jorie noticed Sonny had a photo in his hand. "You taking that with us?"

Sonny looked down at the photo. "Yes, I need to make a stop at the church. I want to speak to my brother."

Yea, that was not going to be a meeting that Jorie wanted to participate in. "Anything I need to be aware of?"

"I'm not sure yet."

That was good enough for Jorie.

Sonny looked down at the photo again then back up at Jorie. "You know I think we can wait and talk to Michael after we interview these other three suspects."

"You want to bring them in for questioning or what?" asked Jorie.

"That will depend on them." Sonny stopped short when he reached his car. Written in what appeared to be red lipstick was one word. PROMISES.

Jorie saw Sonny's face go crimson as he stood by the car. Coming around to the driver's side he could see the word on the window. "Okay Sonny who has a hard on for you right now. This shit is getting crazy. Let's get the forensics team out here."

"Go ahead and call them out."

* * *

Once the forensics team was on site Sonny choose to ride with Jorie. He knew in his gut they wouldn't find any DNA on the car. Whoever this mother fucker was. They would slip up sooner than later Sonny was sure of.

* * *

Lori Hammonds stood across the street from the NOPD watching Sonny and Jorie. She loved seeing him so riled up. Poor, poor Sonny he should have kept the promises he had made.

And that little side kick of his Jorie. She could do without him being always around. She could get rid of him easy enough. That hot little thing he was sleeping with could have a tiny accident.

That would keep Jorie busy for a while. Lori Hammonds stepped out of the store front she was standing in as Jorie's black Camaro drove away. Stepping into the street she dared them to notice her as the car went down the street.

* * *

It turned out James King was a legitimate business man. The only thing it seemed he was guilty of was getting mixed up with a couple of hookers that instead of a good time had drugged him and robbed him.

Poor guy was trying to figure out how he was going to explain to his wife why he was transferring funds from their personal accounts into his travel account. Sonny didn't feel sorry for him. Do the crime, do the time. Was Sonny's motto. They had a bolo out on the couple from Maine. They had checked out of their hotel on Canal street quite hastily.

They would pick them up soon enough. Sonny couldn't put it off any longer he had to go see Michael.

The forensic team had found no DNA just as Sonny had predicted and his car was now clean. Sonny would call ahead and see if his brother wanted lunch.

* * *

Sonny headed out for lunch he had decided to meet Michael at the cathedral, Sonny's brother seemed happy to have lunch with him. Sonny wanted to go back over what happened at the church between the discovery of the slain woman and the police arriving on scene.

Deciding to walk over to the Cathedral Sonny found the weather enjoyable and he was also relieved that he didn't feel like he was being followed.

It took him no time to walk the four blocks over to Jackson Square. Maybe Michael would be willing to go to Muriel's for lunch Sonny had been craving their Shrimp and Grits.

On entering the church Sonny flagged down Sheryl, Michael's secretary. She seemed reluctant to acknowledge him but, still made her way down the aisle to him.

"Sheryl, could you tell me where Michael is?"

Sheryl scrunched her nose as she starred at him Sonny noticed. "Sheryl is there a problem here?"

"No sir. You can follow me. I believe Father Delacroix is in his office."

"Thank you, Sheryl. How are you today?"

Sheryl just silently lead Sonny to the office area. She never answered him. Sonny got the feeling she did not feel comfortable with him.

Sonny went to open Michael's office door as Sheryl creased her brow at him and shook her head. Sonny held his hands up in surrender letting the woman do her job.

Sheryl knocked on the door and only opened it when a come in resinated from behind the closed door.

"Father, Officer Delacroix is here to see you."

Michael stood up and came around his desk smiling at his secretary. "Sheryl, I think you can just say it's my brother."

"Yes Father."

"Sheryl, Sonny and I will be having lunch here would you like to join us?"

Sonny took that moment to interject. "Actually, that would be a good idea. I wanted to go over the events that happened between the time the victim was found and the police arrived."

Sonny noticed his brother's secretary looking a bit agitated at the mention of the crime. "Sheryl is there something wrong?"

"No, and I wouldn't be any help. I wasn't here that morning until sometime after. I was sick that morning."

"Well if you would still like to join us for lunch you can."

Sheryl shook her head and darted out the office.

Sonny looked at his brother, "She's a strange one Michael."

"Sonny, she's just not a woman that falls for the Delacroix charm." Michael laughed and showed Sonny back towards the dining hall.

"I thought perhaps Muriel's for lunch."

"Oh, I don't have that kind of time to be away from the church. Do you mind eating here?"

Sonny shrugged and followed his brother.

*   *   *

All was not lost by having lunch with Michael. It seemed Sonny and Jorie needed to find Mr. Helms. It appeared the man was in the church when the police arrived and asked for a bathroom, then Michael did not recall him coming back to the sanctuary. Sonny would check on the bolo when he got back to the station house.

*   *   *

When Sonny left the station house he headed home once there he showered and dressed for dinner, problem was he didn't have any plans. Grabbing his coat and keys Sonny decided he would have that shrimp and grits

at Muriel's for dinner.

Chapter Seven

Sitting in Muriel's sonny sat back enjoying his scotch. It was rare he felt like having dinner out. Mostly he spent his off time at home. He hated running into people that thought they knew him or wanted something from him. You didn't get to slide through life with a father like Rene Delacroix and not have some form of heartache or inconvenience.

Sonny had carved out a life away from his father's world and made sure everyone knew he was independent despite his last name. Now Sonny sat at his table enjoying his scotch watching a very attractive young woman. She was probably 5'7 nice curves. Pretty green eyes that gleamed as she discussed her point with heated enthusiasm. Sonny smiled to himself what could have her so exasperated.

He didn't mean for his mind to go directly to sex. But, it did the thought of her bent over his bed while he buried his cock in her sweet wet warm pussy had his cock twitching. When she sat across from her friend with her mouth partially opened in surprise he could imagine it wrapped around his cock as well. He could imagine her watching him with those emerald green eyes as he rode her sweet mouth.

Coming out of his thoughts he noticed her looking across the room at him. Sonny smiled and raised his glass to her. When she blushed, and smiled back. He thought if she only knew what he was really smiling about she would definitely not be smiling. Maybe she would get wet if she knew.

Sonny's view disappeared when a shadow cast across his table. Looking up he was surprised by an older woman. Probably in her early sixties.

"Is there something I can help you with?"

"You look like your father. Yes, I knew him well."

"Don't care."

"You should Mr. Delacroix."

Before Sonny could respond she walked off with her much younger escort. When Sonny looked back across the room the attractive brunette was gone. It was probably better she was gone.

"Why do you think it's better that I'm gone?"

Sonny looked up at the attractive young woman and thought did he say that out loud.

"Yes, you spoke out loud." she smiled.

"I suppose I did. Are you sure it's you I was speaking of?"

"I sure hope so."

It seems his night may have a very different ending then what he had expected. Before Sonny could offer her a seat she pulled out the chair next to him and sat down.

"Should I have waited for you to ask me to sit?"

Sonny smiled at her and simply said no. Waving the waiter over he looked back at the young woman who was smiling back at him.

"I'm Sonny."

"Dani. It's nice to meet you Sonny."

As the waiter approached Sonny asked what Dani would like to drink. He watched as she reached over and took his glass. Dani brought the glass to her lips and tasted the scotch. When she finished, she sat the glass down in front of her.

"I have a drink, thank you just the same."

Dani tried not to laugh. She had never in her life acted like this around a man. She was tired of being afraid of not knowing what else was out there, when she looked across the room and saw Sonny staring at her like she was desert her mind went to a place of sheer fantasy and in an instant, she had clinched her thighs together just imagining him slamming her against a wall and fucking her.

Never in her life had she had a man meet her needs fully. She always seemed to find the ones that just wanted to make love to her quote UN quote. If she could just have one night of intense fucking with this man she would be satisfied with the love making boys. Who was she kidding if Sonny did the things she imagined he could do she would be forever ruined for all other.

"I will have another scotch please Justin."

Sonny had no clue what Dani was thinking but, the smile she was trying not to have spread across her face was just enough of a tease to make him want to find out more about her.

"What do you do Dani?"

* * *

I'm sitting right here and he doesn't even know I'm in the room. Was I that forgettable Sonny? What's that little tart have that I don't?

Lori sat at the bar in Muriel's watching Sonny as he eye fucked the little tart that now sat with him drinking out of his glass.

She should leave now go to his house and rip the place part.

Problem with that was she wanted to watch this little scene play out. Would Sonny take her home? That would be so out of the ordinary. Sonny liked his personal life and precise. Lori had deducted that over the years. This was just a new type of game he was playing with his consorts.

If Sonny left with the tart Lori would have to up her game. She was prepared to go all the way to drive Sonny absolutely crazy. Lori was always around to keep Sonny in line. He had made promises and he was going to keep them.

* * *

Sonny listened contently as Dani talked nonstop about everything he couldn't help but smile while he listened. What amazed him was that he actually was paying attention to every word. It seemed she lived in the warehouse district in a third-floor loft apartment and payed way more then what it was worth.

Dani was night classes over at Tulane getting her business degree. She worked as a liquor company representative. Dani had been with the company for ten years, Sonny signaled for the waiter to bring his check.

"Are we leaving?" Dani smiled.

"We are." Sonny answered. Leaning forward he placed his right arm on the table. Sonny eased his left hand up Dani's thigh pushing the thin silky fabric of her dress up so he could caress smooth skin. When she licked her bottom lip, Sonny moved his hand to the inside of the thigh sliding it higher. To his surprise, Dani slid closer towards his hand instead of pushing his hand away.

"Tell me Dani if I wanted to slip my fingers underneath your panties while Justin the waiter approaches the table would you deny me?" Sonny waited for an answer. He didn't wait long as Dani's eyes closed to half mass and she answered no in a husky breath.

God, damn he needed to get them out of here and to his place. About that time, the waiter laid the ticket down and left with a wink. Sonny signed the check never removing his hand from between Dani's quivering thighs. As he added the tip to his bill Sonny brushed his finger against Dani's clit and heard her suck in her breath. When he laid the pen down he looked at her.

"You should know I'm not going to make love to you tonight." Sonny had to smile when Dani's response was a soft oh.

"Yes, Dani I'm going to fuck until you can't walk."

He waited to see her response. Sonny got it when she put her hand over his and pushed it harder against her clit.

"Then I will crawl home well satisfied Sonny."

Slipping his hand from her Sonny stood up buttoning his jacket. Dani caught the undeniable bulged that his coat was about to cover. She wanted to say OMG out loud but let it remain silent. What had she got herself into. She reminded herself this is what she wanted. What she had been looking for. To be with a very capable man that knew how to please her. No to fuck her, Dani could only hope this wasn't a huge mistake.

"Ready Dani?"

Dani took Sonny's hand and let him pull her to her feet. She was thankful he gave her a moment to get her feet underneath her good before he guided her towards the exit. As Dani walked Sonny rested his hand on Dani's lower back letting her know although he was walking beside her Sonny was in control.

"Sonny?"

"Yes Dani?"

Sonny stopped walking to look down at Dani he wanted her to know she had his utmost attention. Her emerald green eyes were wide as she exhaled.

"Dani, just spit it out."

"I never asked you anything about yourself."

Sonny laughed. Placing his hand on her lower back again Sonny continued to guide Dani out the restaurant. "I'm a detective for

New Orleans P.D. I also live in the warehouse district. About five blocks from you. Dani I'm very well known here and about twenty people saw you leave with me."

Dani smiled up at him and continued walking. Her stomach had butterflies going bat shit crazy and her palms were sweating. She kept telling her inner woman that she could do this.

Sonny wanted her stripped naked and begging. It had been a long time since he picked up a woman on a whim. The idea made him a bit apprehensive. Trying not to think about the last woman he had taken to his home without some form of contract had Sonny slowing his pace. It was Dani and her green eyes that snapped him back to the present.

"Sonny do you want to change your mind?"

"No."

Sonny led Dani to his car. He wanted to burn off a little steam before they got to his house. Hopefully Dani wouldn't mind a drive first. Sonny would make sure she enjoyed the ride.

Leading Dani to his car he unlocked the door and opened it watching as her dress slipped up her thighs as she slid in. When she went to pull the dress down Sonny shook his head no and to his surprise she stopped pushing it down and pulled it back up where it was. Sonny cocked his head at her, Dani replied by tugging he dress a little higher. Sonny nodded once and closed the door. This was going to be a fun drive.

Pulling away from the curb Sonny made his way onto Canal Street heading towards I-10. He didn't miss the look Dani gave him as he entered the on ramp for the freeway. Sonny turned the radio on. Dani leaned her head back as the soft sound of Nina Simone whispered out of the speakers.

As the road smoothed out of a deep curve Sonny eased into the middle lane and set the cruise. "Dani, unfastened my slacks."

Dani looked over a bit dazed. She turned in her seat and reached over the console and unbuckled Sony's belt then undid the button and unzipped his pants.

"Take my cock out."

Dani did what he asked she licked her lips as she saw his size. She stroked gently as she looked up at Sonny. Total control was all she saw. Her grip tightened and her stroke quickened s she clinched her thighs together. Her panties were already moist if he would just touch her back. As if he had read her mind Sonny spoke.

"Dani, I want you to stop stroking me and take your panties off. Slid your dress down under your breast."

She did exactly what Sonny had asked her to do. Dani had never been an exhibitionist the thought of people being able to see her was almost liberating almost she thought. Dani waited for Sonny to tell her what he wanted next. She didn't have to wait long.

"That's nice. Now pull the dress up so I can see that sweet pussy."

Dani looked at Sonny as she pulled her dress up. The ways his eyes watched her fingers draw up the dress to expose her to him was exhilarating. Her pussy ached for him to fuck her.

"Slip your shoes off Dani and place your right foot up on the seat."

When she had done what he told her to do she waited for his direction.

"Now open your legs for me."

Sonny's cocked jerked as Dani put her hand back on him. Reaching over Sonny rubbed his fingers against Dani's clit and smiled as she squirmed in her seat. The small moan the escaped her throat had him slipping his fingers deeper into her. Sonny liked the way Dani responded to him. Now he wanted her mouth on him.

Pulling his thumb from her pussy he sucked it into his mouth. She tasted like warm rich honey. Dani moaned and started stroking Sonny's cock faster as he sucked the taste of her off his thumb. Dani couldn't stop her body as she became wet from just the sight of him.

"Get on your knees and lean over the console Dani. I want your mouth on my cock now!"

She only hesitated for a minute looking at the window'

"The windows are too dark for anyone to see us. Now Dani are you going to put hat sweet ass of yours in the air and your mouth on my cock?"

Dani did exactly that her ass had nowhere else to be but in the air as she sucked and licked Sonny's cock. When she felt, his fingers slid down the crease of her ass and he started fingering her the faster he pounded his hand against her pussy the deeper she sucked him down her throat.

She felt the car come to a stop and Dani saw Sonny put the car in park. His free hand tangled in her hair and held her firmly in place as he thrust up into her mouth. Dani came apart again, the dampness that ran along her thighs did so because of the rhythm of Sonny's hand.

Sonny's hand was soaked from Dani's repeated orgasm the sensation of her throaty moans had him thrusting harder into her mouth pushing deep into her throat.

Dani couldn't handle it she needed more Sonny's fingers she wanted them deeper in her. She started riding his fingers faster keeping up with his thrusting cock when the last orgasm hit her it had her mouth stretching open so wide as a strangled cry escaped her throat.

When Dani tried stretching her head back her mouth opened wider and Sonny felt the orgasm that blasted through her and he followed suit holding her head as his cock bucked out as orgasm that flowed down her throat. When he released her hair, Dani licked up Sonny's cock and over the tip before she rested her head on his thigh. Sonny's fingers remained in Dani's soaking wet pussy while he caught his breath.

Both he and Dani were drenched in sweat, breathing ragged. Sonny hadn't lost that kind of control in a long time and he never felt better. Finally having his breathing back under control Sonny slipped his fingers from Dani's body and gentle patted her ass. Next time he might finger her in that sweet ass.

"Dani, you okay?"

Dani just nodded her head against Sonny's thigh she wasn't sure she could actually speak. As Sonny rubbed his hand over ass, her body quivered. There wasn't any way she could be ready to go again.

"Think you can slide your legs off the seat. You can stay where you are if you want." Sonny laughed softly." I like your ass in the air."

"Can I curl up in the seat and keep my head right here?"

Sonny knew it couldn't be comfortable. So, he helped her up right. But, he left her dress bunched around her waist. Pulling the seat belt across her he kissed Dani softly on the mouth as he clicked the belt into place. Sitting back, he admired the sleepy look on her face as he tucked his dick away and fastened his slacks.

"Dani?"

"Hmmm…"

"Home or my place for another round?"

Dani wanted more. She wanted all of him deep in her.

"Another round."

Sonny picked up her hand and held it to his mouth. "Perfect answer."

Sonny pulled the car back onto the highway heading for the closest exit so he could head back to the warehouse district.

Chapter Eight

Lori stood in the dark alcove across the street from Sonny's house in the warehouse district. She had watched him leave with the little tart from Muriel's. Now, where was he? He never picked up women in public places. Had that been an act? Some new game he played?

The cold didn't bother her but Sonny not coming home was pissing her off. If he thought she would allow him to find someone to spend quality time with he was sorely mistaken.

The flash of head lights had Lori stepping further back into the shadows. Smiling to herself she knew he wouldn't stay with the tart. The garage door opened as the Lexus pulled in before the door closed, Lori's smile disappeared into an angry snarl as she watched Sonny get out and walk around the car. As he helped the brunette from the car Lori almost screamed out loud. She didn't miss how the girls dress was barely hanging on her body. She looked like she had been well fucked. That pissed Lori off. "He will learn not to play games with me."

Sonny wrapped Dani's coat around her shoulders, the temperature was dropping quickly and that slinky little dress wasn't keeping her warm. Taking a minute to look down at Dani Sonny couldn't help himself he pressed her against the Lexus's and kissed her roughly. Probably too rough but she needed to know he wasn't a gentle man he wasn't looking to love her tonight what he was going to do was fuck her till she couldn't walk straight.

When he stopped the kiss, he looked her eye to eye. "You sure Dani?"

"Yes."

'I'm not your average guy. I like certain things Dani."

"I need you Sonny any way you come."

Wrapping his arm around her Sonny guided her to the door.

* * *

Lori rolled under the closing garage door silently she lay at the back of Sonny's Lexus. She had been here before, watched him with women before. This bitch was different and she wanted to see.

Smiling to herself. She had always been a voyeur. She liked to watch before she played. This was different, this was fuel to a fire that had started long ago.

* * *

Sonny watched Dani as she walked into his home, slipping his coat off he laid it across the back of a bar stool and loosened his tie. For the first time, he wondered if the woman looking over his home liked what she saw.

Stepping up behind Dani Sonny didn't say anything he simple slipped her coat from her shoulders and turned to lay it aside. Glancing over his shoulder he saw her starring out the living room windows. Her dress hung loosely against her curvy body.

Sonny walked toward the bar. "Dani, would you like a drink?"

"Yes, that would be nice."

Sonny watched as Dani turned and started to walk towards the bar area, he held up his hand for her to stay where she was. Smiling Sonny poured two glasses of scotch. Making his way back to where Dani stood he handed her a glass.

"You have a beautiful home Sonny. I love the view."

Sonny looked her up and down, "I like the view also." he smiled.

Sonny took a seat in one of his club chairs. "Take off your dress." It was a statement not a demand he decided. Although he made the statement firmly, to see what she would do. Sonny was pleased as the dress floated to the floor. "You look splendid in that light." Spinning his finger in the air had Dani smiling as she turned per his instruction.

As Dani turned slowly Sonny removed his tie and unbuttoned the top few buttons of his dress shirt. "Dani, can you come here please?"

Sonny liked how she was quick to oblige him, without question. Holding out his hand Dani slid her hand into his and let Sonny pull her onto his lap. Dani had no other option but to straddle him. Sonny sat their glasses on a side table and before another word was said he took her mouth roughly with his own completely taking her over.

* * *

Lori stood in the darkened doorway as Sonny stood from his chair with the little tart from the restaurant wrapped around him. The tarts Jimmy Choo knock offs were hooked at the back of Sonny's waist as he carried her into his bedroom.

Fucking bitch!! Lori walked over to where the glasses set and picked up Sonny's. Rubbing the rim along her lips she purred quietly at the smell of the scotch and the warmth of the glass against her lips. His lips had caressed the glass she wanted to taste his kiss again. She wanted to taste more than his lips. What did a girl have to do to be noticed by the mighty Sonny Delacroix? Maybe I should become a brunette.

Lori heard the cry of passion coming from the bedroom she couldn't resist the urge to watch so she moved closer to the bedroom's open door. She could see perfectly thanks to the position of Sonny's bureaus mirror.

Sonny had the woman on her back and was already ridding her hard. Her hands gripped his shoulders to the point her nails were digging in his skin. *Is he looking at her while he fucks her? What in the hell he never watches them while he fucks them.* Lori noticed instantly she had missed it. Sonny had her on her back, on her fucking back. Not on her hands and knees like the others. He liked this one. He really liked this one. Sonny was a big on instant attraction. Always said a fucks a fuck but, a connection or attraction meant more. So much more.

When the bitch in the bed cried out for more Lori stepped back as Sonny gave her what she asked for. Sonny never let them control any part of the act. As Lori thought about that one single fact she was already heading back out the house down into the garage. She needed to get out of there fast, before she made a mistake.

* * *

Jorie waved Sonny over as he entered the old Coffee Pot restaurant on St. Peter Street. Sonny made his way through the crowded cafe. He would have preferred staying home a little longer this morning. He would have preferred driving Dani home instead of having to put her in a cab sending her home like she was no more than a one night stand. She wasn't, Sonny was sure of that. Hell, he had given her his number. That was strictly for her to call him to let him know she got home safely. *Sure, it was* he thought that's why he had gotten her number as well.

"What's that smirk on your face about?" asked Jorie as Sonny sat down.

"Nothing."

"Give it up Delacroix."

"Fine, I meet someone last night."

"Who's this someone?"

"Why did you call me out this early?"

Jorie got to the point as the waitress came over to pour more coffee and take their order.

"We got a hit on the bolo on the Helms couple. They are bringing them in."

"Then why are we sitting here having breakfast?"

"Settle down Sonny. They were picked up in Lake Charles. It will be a few hours before they get to the station. SO, have some coffee and tell me about this woman you have met."

Sonny sipped his coffee. He smiled at Jorie and said nothing. Sonny thought for a minute that Jorie would explode if he didn't tell him something. So, he gave him Dani's name and a few details. When Jorie laughed out loud and told him it was good to see him smiling again. Sonny almost got up and left but, for whatever reason he did not.

"I'm glad this delights you Jorie. How's my sister?"

"She wasn't feeling good this morning. She even looked a little green. She said if it didn't pass she was going to the walk-in clinic."

"Should I call and check in. Maybe have mom go by."

"If Raya calls and says she still feels bad I will let you know and mama Del can go over and take care of our girl."

Sonny agreed. Lord knew his mother could be a blessing and a curse. The waitress rushed over to their table flustered.

"Excuse me detective, there was a shady looking character messing with your car."

"My car Jorie?" Asked Jorie jumping up.

"No, his." the waitress pointed at Sonny. Who didn't hesitate as he headed out the door into the street. Walking around his car he found not one but two flat tires. At closer inspection, they had been slashed. Jorie just looked around, his hand on his gun as he called the precinct.

"Dispatch is sending a tow truck. Where do you want, it sent?"

"I will send it to Mikie's."

* * *

It didn't help Sonny's mood when the Mr. Helms turned out to be no more than a high-end fence. Poor guy probably would never come back to New Orleans again after experiencing an interrogation from the likes of Sonny.

Sonny was never more ready for the day to end then he was for this one to. Heading out he meet Jorie out front.

"Thought you might want a ride home."

"Thanks. What kind of plans you and Raya have for the weekend?"

"Laying low until mass on Sunday and then to your moms for lunch. What about you?"

"Have a few things to do around the house."

"You seeing your new friend this weekend?" Jorie laughed.

Sonny made no comment as he got into Jorie's car. He knew anything he said would just have Jorie asking more questions than he was ready to answer. Instead he turned on the radio and listened to the radio silently.

Sonny waved as Jorie drove off. Sonny wanted the quite of his home. He had brought the case files home to go over yet again. He hadn't made any plans for the weekend so why not do some work he had thought. There was a coupe games on this weekend and he needed to do some work around his place.

The fridge was stocked and pizza was only a phone call away if he decided he wasn't in the mood to cook

* * *

I'm tired of seeing them traipse in and out. I told him they shouldn't be here. I told him not to play with them, he will learn. He will listen to me. I will teach them and him a lesson.

He knows he should listen when I say I am watching him.

Chapter Nine

Sonny sat at the back of the church for morning mass on Sunday. He had wanted to come to early mass so he could get a few things together before he went to his moms for lunch.

It was more a ritual than anything. The whole family congregated at Mama Delacroix's on Sunday's. You never know who would show up. Some folks just stop in for a cup of coffee or a slice of cake. Some came and stayed all day.

After mass Sonny headed home to change and grab grocery's his mom had asked him to bring. Which was his pasta and meat sauce. Everyone chipped in for Sunday meals.

* * *

Michael was in his office about to change when a knock came at his door. He usually had time to go home and change but today he had lead two services and was about to run late getting to his mothers.

"Come in."

"Father I am sorry to bother you. I was wondering if you would like to have lunch with me. We have not had time to really talk since that poor woman was found dead."

Michael noticed Sheryl seemed out of sorts the past week. He felt bad for the woman. "Sheryl, why don't you come to dinner at my mothers with me today. I think you could use being around some people. And my mom would love to have you over.

"Will your brother be there?"

"Which one are you referring to?"

Sheryl looked confused at Michael's statement. "You have more than one?"

Michael smiled. "Yes, I have two, not counting Jorie Michaels. He's more like a pet." Michael laughed at his joke that Sheryl clearly missed.

"Why don't you wait for me out in the front office I will only be a couple minutes."

Sheryl agreed and closed the door behind her as she left his office.

* * *

When Sonny finally arrived, he was not surprised by how many people were at his mother's house but who. There was one person in particular he was surprised to see. That was Sheryl his brother's secretary.

Walking into the kitchen he said his hellos and accepted hugs and kisses and even a few pinches on his cheeks from a few aunts. Finally having his hands free he turned to find he was alone in the kitchen with non-other than his brothers secretary.

"Sheryl, how are you today?"

Sheryl speaking softly replied she was fine and thanked Sonny for asking before she dashed out of the kitchen. Sonny closed his eyes breathing deeply.

"You trying to center yourself big brother?"

"Raya, when did you get here?"

"I was already here. Just in the bathroom."

Sonny held his sister back by her shoulders as he searched her face for clues. "You feeling okay?"

"Yes. Why?"

"Jorie said you weren't feeling well on Friday."

"I'm good."

Sonny and Raya's conversation ended abruptly when two aunts came bustling into the kitchen with more dishes in their hands. Everyone was shooed from the kitchen except for the elders. That meant food was about to be set out.

When Sonny and Raya entered the living room there were a few extra people than before, A few beat cops and one or two other detectives had stopped by. It was not uncommon for police officers to stop by. The Delacroix house was known to take in strays and feed the hungry especially cops.

As everyone settled in while they waited for dinner to be served the conversation covered everything from how the Saints were doing this season to who served the best poboy in town. When the conversation came back around to work, the topic of the murder came up. There were a lot of speculation of who could have done it to why they did it. None of which was helpful.

The thing that Sonny noticed was that Sheryl seemed nervous. She rubbed her hands together over and over.

He watched as she rubbed her closed hand across her mouth, she continued to fidget in her chair. When the kitchen door swung over she jolted from her seat almost tumbling to the floor. Michael who had been standing next to her managed to grab her and help her get her balance.

"Are you okay?"

"Yes, father. I just was so engrossed in the topic I was startled by the noise."

"If you're sure you are okay."

Sheryl smiled but, the smile did not reach her eyes. Sonny knew Michael noticed it also.

"What is the problem in here?" asked Mama Delacroix.

"We were discussing the case."

"What case?" she asked.

The younger beat cop missed Sonny's subtle nod to not tell her. When he turned, and answered her. Sonny was sure he realized his mistake immediately.

Mama Delacroix wiped her hands on her apron as she walked fully into the room. "I will not have that case discussed in my house. I will not have it discussed ever in this house and most certainly not on Sunday. DO I make myself clear?"

The room was quiet. There would be no more talk of murder in that house on that day. It was Jorie who broke the tension.

"Hey who brought the Cannoli?"

Raya threw a pillow at him. The conversation started back up except for the taboo topic. But, Sonny kept his eye on his brother's secretary the rest of the day. She appeared to be following the conversation but she averted the simplest questions about herself unless she was questioned again.

Sonny made mental notes of all the information she gave up. It wasn't much but it was things he could quietly and with ease check out without having to alert anyone he was considering her background. Something was just off about the woman.

As the afternoon wore on the crowd trickled down in the Delacroix house. Sonny liked it when it became just family. At least until the mention of his older brother came up. Francis his older brother made his decision to leave the family. Sonny for one would not sit here another Sunday while his mother praised Francis.

"It's time for me to go. Mom thank you for a lovely afternoon." Sonny kissed his mom and headed for the door. Jorie walked out with him. "What car are you in?"

"My backup."

"No way. You brought the vet out?"

"I do take it out every now and again Jorie."

"Man, I have to look at it. Come on hand over the keys."

"No way. You can just look but you don't touch son." Sonny laughed as Jorie jogged down the driveway to look at the other love of his life. Jorie had loved the vet ever since Sonny bought it when they were in their teens. It had been a wreck and Sonny had taken his sweet time restoring it. Very rarely did he take it out.

"Ya know Delacroix when I marry your sister this car is mine."

"In your dream's, Michaels."

"Not true big brother. If I remember when I was little you told Jorie the day he married me would be the day you let him have your car."

Raya laughed as she jogged down the driveway towards Jorie. Leaving Sonny standing with his mouth hanging open.

Chapter Ten

four weeks later:

Sheeting rain slammed against the streets of the city, *what a day* Sonny thought as he drove to 1001 Chartres St. Pulling up in front of the hotel Sonny peered out the car window. Damn it he cursed stepping out of the Lexus into the down pour. Quickly stepping into the alcove adjoining the lobby to the side rooms he shook the rain from his coat before entering the hotel lobby.

Jorie stepped up into Sonny's line of vision. "Nice of you to meet us."

Sonny cocked a look at him that said clearly to fuck off. "What do we have?"

"Always so serious brother."

"Nothing funny about murder Jorie."

Signaling with his hand Jory pointed in the direction of the murder scene. A beat cop stepped up holding an umbrella over he and

Sonny. "Please tell me the body is in a room and not out in the weather Jorie."

"It isn't in the weather nor a room. It's in the back staircase."

Following Jorie into the hallway with the winding staircase sonny looked up. "What floor?"

"First landing."

Climbing the stairs, it only took a couple steps to see the woman staring out of the window. "Who let her up here?"

"Oh her, she is the victim."

Looking back at Jorie he watched as he shrugged. It seemed the woman had been staged kneeling looking out the first-floor stairwell window. The coroner was on scene, maybe they would have a time of death.

"Before you get up there Sonny there's something you should know."

Stopping Sonny looked back at Jorie. "What's that?"

Taking a deep breath Jorie spoke, "She has her rosary laced through her fingers."

Rubbing a hand over his face Sonny turned and hustled up the stairs. Coming to the top he saw Joe working on the body. "Joe what do we have."

Joe was a looker with cascading auburn hair that hung in a riot of natural curls down her back and alarming blue eyes. Every guy in the precinct probably took a chance asking her out but Joe was happily married since a year out of high school. Jason was everything the woman loved and adored. Turning to look at Sonny she gave a nod and stood up.

"Well she was strangled I'm guessing sometime around four a.m."

"Was she brought here or killed here?

"That's not my job Sonny. That's yours. "Joe smiled as she moved away from victim. "Gentlemen." She nodded and let the Detectives have the scene.

"Who found the body?"

"One of the maids she's being detained in the front office."

"Okay let's go over what we know."

What they knew was only the victim had been strangled and her prayer beads had been wrapped around her neck. There seemed no clues to whether she had been killed in the staircase or somewhere else. Forensic would be combing the area but too Sonny it seemed not to be any unless it was on the victim or underneath her.

Two victims down, one more and this would become a serial killer case and the FBI would be called in. When he and Jorie had started going over the files that had been sent to them about the church pew strangler they were sure it was the same killer until they saw a difference it was a small difference but it was one all the same.

All the other victims the rosary beads had been placed around the throats of the victims these two murders the rosary were placed in their hands. Could the killer have changed that small detail just to throw them off the trail or was it a completely new killer on the loose?

Damn Sonny had hoped it was just a simple strangling two weeks ago but now it looked like it was more. As Sonny moved around the scene he caught a familiar odor. A perfume. "Joe, the victim she wearing perfume?"

"Yes, honeysuckles it smells like. Why?"

"Just asking."

Sonny walked up the next flight of stairs. Following his nose. The scent disappeared. Making his way back down to talk to Jorie. His thoughts were somewhere else.

As they finished the interview with the hotel staff. Jorie walked Sonny out. The rain had stopped, but it left a brutal cold in its wake.

"You seeing Dani this weekend?"

"I'm not sure. She has exams."

"You know that sounds funny?"

"Only because your juvenile Jorie."

"Maybe we can go out to dinner with the two of you."

"I'll see. Now can we get back to this case?"

Jorie nodded. They both knew this was going to be another long day.

* * *

Back at the precinct Sonny looked over both sets of crime scene photos. His gut told him he had missed something important. He just couldn't put his finger on it.

"You going over those photos again Sonny?"

"I missed something."

"Sonny, come on how many times have you looked at that first crime scene. A hundred times? If there were something to see you would have seen it."

Sonny tossed the photos on his desk causing some to fall on the floor. When Jorie picked them up he noticed two photos were stuck together. Peeling them apart Jorie saw what

Sonny was looking for. Handing the photo to Sonny he waited only a moment.

In the new-found photo, Sonny saw someone who said she was not present at the church during the events. Sheryl Daniels had lied. The picture said so. On the very edge of the photo she stood hugging a door frame, the expression on her face was fear.

He had known something was off with her but, why hadn't he checked her out. His brother that's why. "Jorie, we need to find out everything we can on Sheryl Daniels. You know the drill. I want everything we can find on her before I pick her up.

* * *

Sonny found Michael in the assembly. He really did not want to have this conversation with his brother but the fact was that Sheryl Daniels hadn't existed until three years ago.

Sonny had noticed her odd behavior any time he was near. Especially if he had questions about the morning of the first murder.

"Michael."

Father Michael Delacroix turned at the sound of his name being called out. Turning he frowned looking at his brother. He was thankful no one happened to be in the church. Shaking his head as he met Sonny in the aisle.

"Sonny keep your voice down, you're in church."

Looking around he cocked an eye at his brother. "Yea I see its crowded."

"Do not be like that. Now what bring you in again?"

"Sheryl. Where is your secretary?"

"Probably in the office. Why do you want to know, Sonny?"

"I need to speak with her. Now!"

"What about Sonny?" Michael asked as he led Sonny toward the office's.

Sonny didn't answer as they walked through the church in to the back area where the office was.

"Sonny. Answer me."

"I just have a few questions for her."

Sonny followed his brother to the office area of the church where they found Sheryl Daniels mat her desk.

"Sheryl, Det. Delacroix would like to speak with you."

The timid secretary looked up at Father Delacroix. Nodding her head, she stood. Sonny watched as her hands began to twitch she clutched them together when she noticed Sonny watching.

"How can I help you Detective?"

"Miss Daniels, you told the officers you were not at the crime scene. This picture says you were. Would you care to explain?"

Sheryl just stared at the photo in Sonny's hand. When she didn't say anything, Sonny asked her to turn around. He began reading her rites as he hand cuffed her.

"Sonny, my god is that necessary." asked Michael.

Sheryl pleaded with Sonny to not take her in that she would answer his questions.

Sonny taking a deep breath took the cuffs off. But, had Jorie escort her to the precinct. Before he left he informed his brother that Miss Daniels hadn't existed until three years ago. Before that who knew. Sheryl Daniels had questions to be answered.

"Michael, if you want to help your secretary I suggest you get her a lawyer." Sonny walked out of his brother's office following behind Jorie and Miss Daniels.

* * *

Sheryl had been placed in an interrogation room where she had sat for close to an hour waiting for someone to come speak with her. When Sonny finally came in she asked to make a call. Sonny informed her she was not under arrest she got up and proceeded to leave,

"Miss Daniels, I just want to speak with you about your whereabouts on a couple of evenings."

"Not without my phone call."

Sonny allowed Sheryl to make the call, he handed her his personal phone. "Miss

Daniels Father Delacroix is already on his way down.

The only person she knew was father Delacroix so she called his office. When Father Delacroix didn't pick up she handed the phone back to Sonny. Sonny didn't touch the phone. He now had her finger prints.

"Sheryl, I don't want to keep you here any longer then needed. I just have a few questions."

"Then please ask them so I can leave."

"You were clearly there the morning of the murder why didn't you tell us that?"

Sheryl let out a breath. "I got there during the ciaos. I had no idea what was happening. I remained in the doorway because I was afraid."

"Afraid of what?"

"I had no idea what was happening. I thought someone was trying to take people hostage or something. I was already in the doorway; my intentions were to call for help. That's when I saw Father Delacroix consoling Ms. Troxclair. I decided to leave and come back when things had calmed down. I had no idea a woman had been murdered till later that morning."

Sonny wasn't buying the story. It was time he put his cards on the table. "We know your real name is not Sheryl Daniels. Your real name is Selena Lowery. You were born in Jackson Mississippi. Your mother died in a car accident when you were thirteen. You were raised by your cousin Linda Reed in Maryland. Would you like to start over?"

Sheryl folded her hands neatly in her lap as she began to speak once more to Sonny. "I'm hiding from a life I would like not to catch up with me. Can we leave it at that?"

"I'm sorry but, no."

Sheryl decided her best bet would be to just come clean with Sonny. She would probably lose her job and must move again. It was looking like she needed to move again anyway. The police on the east coast had never believed her and the same thing was about to happen here. "Yes, my real name is

Selena Lowery. Detective, I have cousin his name is Greg Reed. His mother was my cousin on my mother's side."

"Your records show that you were raised by Linda Reed in Maryland. It also says your cousin Linda had no son."

"Yes, I know what it says about her having a son or not having a son. It also says I suffer from delusional episodes or even schizophrenia. Although I have never been diagnosed. My cousin Linda did have a son, she kept him at home he was troubled."

Sonny would go along with Sheryl/Selena to get to the truth. "Let's say Linda did have a son. What happened to this cousin Greg?"

There had been a fire. The Detectives could easily find that information out. Why had they not at this point was mote. "I thought for years he died in the house fire that killed his mother. But then he found me. I put a restraining order on him but they couldn't find any record of him."

"How do you explain that everywhere you have lived there has been a strangling exactly as the ones we have had here?" Yes, Sonny and Jorie had dug up everything they could find on Miss Daniels/Lowery.

"It's him. I'm telling you its Greg. I think he killed his mother and set the house fire to cover his crime. Every woman looks similar? Det. Delacroix, do they all look somewhat a like?"

"Yes, and they all have red glass rosary beads on their person when they are found."

Sheryl put her head in her hands. It was Greg and he had found her again. This was it, her last chance to have someone stop him to help her out of this nightmare. "Please, I'm begging you. Find him, he won.t stop killing. No one has ever believed me. It's the truth."

"Miss Daniels where were you on the night of November 12th?"

"In my room at the Cheatue hotel."

"Any witnesses?"

"No."

"What about the morning of December 3rd between 12:30 am and two am?"

"At home."

"Witnesses?"

"No."

"That's not true. Said Father Delacroix as he entered the room."

"What are you doing father? This is an interrogation." The last thing Sonny needed was family interfering with the investigation.

"I'm here as a witness for Miss Daniels."

Sonny rose from his chair, meeting his brother as Michael burst into the interrogation room. "What the fuck are you doing Michael. I'm in the middle of an interview!"

"No Sonny you're in the middle of an interrogation. And I won't have it Sheryl is entitled to a lawyer."

It was Sheryl who calmed he situation down. "It's okay Father please have a seat."

Sonny should thank the woman for keeping the peace.

"Sheryl it's going to be okay." Sonny heard his brother tell her. What was going on with Michael and this woman? "What are you doing here Father Delacroix?"

"I am here to clear up a few things. On the night of December 3rd. I was worried about Miss Daniels and traveled to her home. She was there alone."

"You were at her home between 12:30 and 2 am? Doing what Father?" Sonny's curiosity had peaked.

Michael cleared his throat before he spoke again. He knew what he was about to say would bring more questions than he wanted to answer. Sheryl needed him to help her even if she had never asked for it. "I was outside at 1 am and no I didn't knock or go in. I saw her through the window. She was packing a suitcase and then she sat down and began to cry. I felt like it would be wrong to intrude on her, So I went back to my car and sat for a while trying to decide what to do. Her lights went out around 1:30

and I left. So she couldn't have murdered the woman at the hotel."

"What do you mean you sat in your car and saw her lights go out? She lives in a hotel."

Sheryl was dumbfounded by Michaels admission. She barely realized she answered Sonny's question. "No I moved into an apartment a few weeks ago. I live in Kenner off Power Blvd. I take the bus in every day."

"Michael." was all she said as he rose from the table and stared down his brother in her defense.

"If that is all Detective, I will take Miss Daniels home."

Sonny had nothing else for the moment. "Miss Daniels your free to go but, don't leave town. I will be looking into this cousin you claim is our killer." Sonny knew all about people being misdiagnosed first hand. He would keep surveillance on Sheryl.

Chapter Eleven

Dani and Sonny walked down Orleans ave. Headed to meet Jorie and Raya at the Grapevine. Sonny smiled as she told him about acing her exams. He was happy for her. Dani deserved a wonderful job. He hoped she would stay in state but her options were wide open.

When the conversation ended, he took the opportunity to speak. "Thank you for coming to dinner."

"I'm glad you asked me Sonny. I missed seeing you this week."

Sonny only smiled as he opened the restaurant door. They found Raya and Jorie at a table in the far corner of the room. The place was small. It had an exceptional wine selection hence the name.

Raya smiled and rose to her feet to hug both Sonny and Dani telling her how wonderful it was to finally meet her. Dani agreed and that was how it went the rest of the evening right up to the check being laid on the table which Sonny picked up against Jorie's wishes. The look Sonny gave him shut him up fast.

As goodbyes were given and the couples went the opposite directions Sonny wrapped an arm around Dani bringing her in close. "I have a surprise for you tonight. That's if you don't have to go home."

Dani looked up at him. "I'm all yours."

The mile on her face said it all for Sonny. Sonny's car was parked a block up. Making their way to his car the conversation remained easy, and simple. Sonny liked feeling relaxed. Opening the door for Dani he waited for her to get in when she leaned over the door he smiled leaning down to plant a kiss on her, knowing that was what she was aiming for.

*   *   *

I thought this little tart would have been gone by now. What does she have that I don't? She needs to go so you can pay more attention to me Sonny. Lori leaned against a vacant doorway watching Sonny plant a kiss on Dani's lips. She thought he would have ended this fling.

She would have to up the ante. Lori knew what he liked and the little brunette couldn't hold a candle to her. He Just needed to have a clear view of what and who he needed.

Lori watched the car drive off. She had somewhere to be tonight. If she did not show her plans would come to an end.

* * *

Sonny took immense pleasure from the look on Dani's face as they walked into the suit at the Roosevelt Hotel. He had made all the arrangement's a couple weeks ago pending her class finals which he had every reason to have faith she would pass.

Sonny led her further into the room where a bottle of champagne was chilling. He had fresh fruit brought in along with cheese and cracker trays. Sonny wanted her to enjoy her entire evening. That meant doing whatever Dani wanted.

"Sonny you shouldn't have done all this."

"Why not?" Sonny brushed her hair back from her shoulders. Her green eyes danced. You make me happy Dani, I just want to make you happy. Is that so bad?"

"No." she smiled.

"Tonight, it's all about you and what you want to do tonight. So, tell me what would you like to do?"

Sonny knew he was in trouble when she smiled. He watched as she darted through the bedroom and then he heard her scream. Not a scream as in bad but as in good. Sonny rubbed a hand over his face. He knew she found the garden tub. The only thing that made it okay was when she appeared it the door way wearing just her beautiful smile.

"You want to join me in here? I'm running a bath."

Sonny slipped out of his suit jacket and loosened his tie as he started walking towards her. As Dani backed up, as Sonny advanced on her she giggled. Dani liked the slow strip tease Sonny was attempting.

When he unbuckled his belt, Dani stopped laughing and licked her lips. Sonny took that as an invitation and tossed her over his shoulder, heading for the bathroom and a large garden tub which was filling up with warm water.

Sonny knew he surprised the hell out of her when he stepped right in still wearing his pants. He couldn't help but laugh along with Dani as she laughed hysterically. As Sonny sank down with Dani wrapped around him. The kisses Dani rained down on him had him craving more than just her kisses.

*   *   *

Standing looking out the suite's windows Sonny didn't hear Dani slip out of the bed. It startled him when her arms came around him. She said nothing just rested her head against Sonny's chest. Kissing the top of her head. "Did I wake you?"

"No, I just got cold, noticed you weren't in the bed."

Sonny led Dani back to bed and crawled in with her. "Let's see what we can do about warming you up."

Chapter Twelve

The day had been perfect as Sonny walked with Jess down Royal street. It was his first trip home on leave in over a year, her laugh was maddening of infectious depending on how you looked at it. It was late in the evening as they walked along the darkened streets of the city. Why had he agreed to going out so late? Sonny had agreed because it was Jess and he would do whatever she waned, agree to anything she asked for. So, when she asked him if he would love her and only her forever he had said yes. When she told him to promise he had. Now he watched her laugh and dance down the deserted street.

When Jess slipped around a corner laughing he quickened his pace to catch up. Sonny caught sight of her heading into an alley between two buildings. Jogging up to the alley Jess reached out pulling him into the darkness.

"Sonny, I want you…. now, please now."

"Jess, not here baby."

Laughing she nuzzled into him. "Why not?"

"Because someone could see."

Sliding her hand down over his erection she smiled, "that's what makes it hotter. The chance of getting caught."

Looking down at her Sonny's eyesight was adjusting to the dark. "take off your panties and give them to me."

"I'm not wearing any."

"Undo my jeans."

He felt her hands reach up to unbutton his jeans. Pushing his hands in her hair he gripped her tight dragging her head back so her mouth titled up to his." Now Jess, I want you to stroke me."

She followed his directions without hesitation. Stroking his cock, he slammed his mouth over hers the rougher he kissed her the harder she gripped him and her rhythm quickened. Sonny picked her up, Jess wrapped her legs around his waist as he thrust up into her. Twisting around Sonny pushed her up against the brick wall behind them.

When his name came from her on a breathy moan, he thrust harder, his rhythm quickening. Her moans making Sonny loose more control. Keeping her against the wall Sonny pulled at her blouse, when the buttons popped off pinging against the ground she began begging. Rolling her nipple between his fingers had her crying out.

"Quite Jess or I stop."

"Jess tilted her head back against the wall trying to stay silent. As Sonny kept his thrust fast and hard she began to force him to go faster. She was so close she needed more.

"Harder Sonny please harder I need it so bad Sonny!"

Sliding his hand to her throat Sonny held her against the wall as he slowed the pace.

"No, no, no don't stop god don't stop !!"

Sonny pulled out and turned her towards the wall so fast she almost fell off her heels. Grabbing her hand's he placed them on the wall above her head and pulled her ass out towards him. Shoving her skirt up onto her back he shoved her thighs apart.

"Wider Jess."

He liked how well she complied. "Now remember you asked for it." he whispered.

It was the last thing she heard as he shoved his cock balls deep into her throbbing sex and pounded into her without mercy even after she couldn't hold herself up he held her against the wall and continued to fuck her. When his body finally climaxed, he continued until he was drained completely. Leaning into her as she was pressed against the rough wall.

"I love you Jess."

"Love you too."

Sonny woke drenched in sweat, God Damn It! he cursed. Ever since the scene at the hotel when he caught the faint smell of perfume a perfume that Jess had worn. It had been the third time he smelled the perfume. Since then Sonny had started imagining he saw Jess and had started dreaming of her almost every night. Sonny didn't need this shit in the middle of a case.

Laying there Sonny tossed the sheet off his naked body. His hand went to his cock and began a smooth steady rhythm. His thoughts were on a raven haired beauty with an infectious laugh and eyes like honey. As Sonny thought about Jess the images in his mind slipped from Jess to Dani. He could feel her breath on his skin as she kissed her way from his neck to his cock. Her moans fogged his mind. Dani's smell was everywhere. Sonny pumped his fist up and down as his mind reminded him of the way Dani rode him hard and fast. Her breast bouncing as her ass slapped down on his thighs. Sonny could feel the tightening of her pussy as she climaxed.

Sonny thought of Dani drench in sweat trying to give him more then what she had the energy left to do so. Sonny had held her hips tight holding her in place as he ground up into her watching as her head fell back and her fingers rubbed over her nipples. The climax hit Sonny harder than he expected it to. His back bowed as his whole body bucked. Sonny dropped to the bed trying to catch his breath.

Sonny draped his free arm over his eyes and continued to even out his breathing. The phone on the night stand rang startling him. Grabbing it with his free hand he cleared his throat before answering.

"Delacroix."

"Sonny, it's Dani. I wanted to invite you to dinner tonight. That's if you're not busy."

Sonny lay there listening to her voice and his cock twitched.

"I could eat."

Dani listened as Sonny told her he could eat. Fuck her she wanted to have him eat her for breakfast, lunch and dinner. She noticed his voice was rough sounding. Oh, god had she interrupted him with another woman.

"You sound busy. I can call back later."

"I was busy. I'm not now. Do you want to know what I was doing Dani?"

She shouldn't ask him but, damn it she wanted to know. "Yes." she breathed out.

"I was thinking about you, while I stroked my cock."

Dani didn't say anything her free hand was already between her legs as she listened to his voice.

"Dani, did you hear me?"

"Yes." was all she could get out as she rubbed her clit.

"Dani, what do you think about that?"

Her reply was a soft moan. As she pressed harder. Dani couldn't help herself as she moaned into the phone her mind had blanked out on her and her body throbbed. She heard him then.

"Rub harder baby, do it for me. Come on Dani, harder baby." Sonny listened as Dani moaned over and over he knew she was close he could tell by her ragged breathing. "Come on baby I hear you. I love the way you sound when you get off. How wet you get for me."

Dani cried out his name as she came. When her climax settled, she whispered his name.

"Dani."

"Sonny,"

"You better be ready to do that again for me tonight right after fucking dinner."

"Anything you want Sonny."

Sonny didn't think he just spoke and what came out of his mouth surprised him. "Why don't you just pack a bag and come straight over. We can hold up in my place, order takeout and stay in bed all weekend." Sonny waited as silent filled the phone line. Finally, Dani spoke.

"I'm on my way."

"I'll be waiting."

"Sonny?"

"Yes."

"Just unlock the door and get back in bed."

Sonny didn't get a chance to answer, before Dani hung up the phone. "Okay, well this is new territory." sonny spoke out loud. He stretched out on his bed and burst out laughing. He felt like things were clicking in place for him. He was happier than he had been in years. Jorie was right it wasn't his fault what had become of Jess. Surely, she would want him happy. Sonny had spent his life trying to keep promises to a woman that had never kept one she had made to him. Promises that a young foolish boy had made.

* * *

Lori Hammonds drove through the city streets. Her destination, Sonny Delacroix's house. She was tired of seeing him traipse around with Dani Richard. Yes, she had found out all about the little bitch taking up Sonny's time.

She had Sonny acting out of character. Lori wanted him miserable and hurting, not happy and smiling. Sonny had made promises to a girl and he should keep them.

Loving someone else was not going to happen.

This day had been coming for years. Lori just needed to get things in order before she confronted Sonny Delacroix about his lies. She thought when she arrived back in town Sonny would have moved on from the little tart. But, no he was in deeper than before. He had stopped seeing other women. That was a clear sign something had change.

Well everything was about to change. Lori turned, heading up the street to Sonny's house as she was slowing down to park a black mini cooper darted into his drive. Lori parked and watched Dani get out what appeared to be an overnight bag and then she just walked up the stairs and entered the house without hesitation.

Lori lost all control at that moment slamming her fist against the steering wheel until they bleed. Pulling at her own hair, her wig came off revealing her shaved scarred head. When Lori saw her reflection in the mirror she froze and grabbed the wig. Calming instantly, she put the wig back on.

Tears ran down her face as she put the SUV in gear and pulled away slowly. "I will take care of you Sonny. Just you wait. This isn't over."

* * *

Dani entered Sonny's house without hesitation and it felt wonderful. She knew with a man like Sonny she shouldn't let her self-fall so hard, so fast but, damn it she wanted it. Dani was falling fast for the handsome detective. She hoped he was falling just as hard and fast.

Sonny looked up as Dani walked in completely naked the only thing that adorned her body were the thigh high black leather boots with four inch heels. As she ran her hand over her breast and down her stomach Sonny stroked his cock. She wanted to play okay they would play. Sonny would let her have a little control this time.

Dani walked slowly over to the bed. She slowly crawled on the bed and ran her tongue from Sonny's thigh up to his chest where she sucked a nipple into her mouth and racked her teeth across the hard nipple.

Sonny fought the urge to put her on her knees and tie her hands to his bed. He told himself let her have this. When she settled between his thighs, moving his hand from his cock Dani wrapped her mouth around it and began an onslaught of sucking and licking. Sonny reached up and gripped the bottom of the head board trying not to take control. Her mouth on his cock felt like heaven. It took everything in Sonny not to grab her by the hair, hold her in place and fuck her mouth.

Sonny opened his eyes when Dani stopped and crawled up his body. "I like this look on you."

"What look is that, Sonny questioned in a gravelly voice."

"Complete trust in me." Dani told him as she slowly slid her body down his hard cock. "You don't mind if I enjoy this ride do you Sonny."

"You better make it a good ride or it will be the last time you drive. "Sonny smiled as he shoved up into her. Dani sucked her breath in. Sonny played dirty in the bedroom and she loved it.

* * *

Sonny and Dani had stayed in bed all day or at least until they could not stand the phone continuously ringing. Sonny finally answered it with a clipped tone. It had been Raya on the line wanting to come by. She needed to talk to Sonny and it was important.

Sonny would kill Jorie if he broke up with Raya or caused her any heartache what so ever. Sonny and Dani jumped in the shower to get cleaned up which ended up with another round of hot and heavy sex. Sonny had barely gotten jeans on when Raya and Jorie walked in the house.

"What, you don't knock?"

Jorie looked back at the door, "it was open."

Before Sonny could respond Dani walked up next to him smelling like heaven. "I know I closed the door when I came in earlier."

Sonny put an arm around her rubbing her back. "If anyone came in before now they got an ear full." He teased.

Jorie and Raya just looked at Sonny as he laughed softly while he leaned down and kissed Dani.

"Did you guys bring food?" asked Sonny as he pulled Dani over to the sofa and dropped down on it with her tumbling into his lap.

"We ordered pizza before we left my place."

"What are you looking at Raya?" Sonny eyed his baby sister.

"You, big brother and …well the both of you. I haven't seen this side of you … never."

Sonny smiled at his sister. "Get used to it."

Dani smiled as she snuggled deeper into Sonny's bare chest. She would do her very best to keep that smile on his face. Dani sat up as she realized how hard she had fallen. She loved him!!

Sonny watched Dani as she abruptly sat up and looked at him like a deer caught in head lights. "Dani, everything alright. What's wrong baby?"

Dani blurted out the words before her brain said stop …" I love you." Dani scrambled from Sonny's lap and began to pace around the room her hand came to her mouth as she thought about the implications of her words. Then Sonny stopped her, turned her to face him and kissed her stupid. He didn't say he loved her back but he didn't tell her to leave. He drew her into him wrapping his arms around her, nuzzled his face in her hair and whispered thank you in her ear. When she looked up she could have sworn Sonny's eyes were shinny with tears. Before she could make another move the pizza delivery guy knocked on the open door.

"We should probably remember to close that door", came a choked response from Raya.

Dani held on to Sonny longer then she meant to. It was just such a private moment that had been shared with an audience she wasn't sure if her next move.

Knowing Dani was still unsettled over the confession, Sonny kiss the top of her head and drug her to grab plates for the food.

*   *   *

Lori sat outside Sonny's house in a rental car waiting for an opportunity to confront Sonny. She had noticed the door a jar earlier but had heard the two love birds fucking and went back to the car. Lori wanted to confront Sonny alone. So, know she sat and waited while his family visited. Lori had hoped it would be a quick visit. When the pizza delivery truck pulled up Lori decided she would come back later. YOU, will be alone sooner than later Delacroix.

*   *   *

As pizza was consumed and the conversation between Sonny and Jorie went into a discussion of the strangler case. Dani and Raya retired to the living room to watch a movie.

Sonny looked at Jorie and quietly asked him what was going on. Raya had sounded nervous and anxious on the phone. Before Jorie could answer Raya was up off the sofa running for the guest bathroom and Jorie was right behind her.

Sonny and Dani crammed in the doorway of the bathroom were engulfed in concern as Raya threw up every ounce of pizza she had eaten earlier.

"Do we need to go to the clinic Raya?' Sonny was more than just concerned, Raya had never been one to get sick. Now that he looked at her she looked thin. He watched as Jorie handed her a cold wash cloth for her face.

"This is not how I pictured telling you that you're going to be an uncle." Raya frowned waiting for a screaming fit from her brother what she got surprised her.

Sonny moved Jorie out of his way as he settled on the floor next to his baby sister. Rubbing her back, he smiled at her. "Are you happy?" When Jorie went to answer, Sonny looked at him with a stern look. Jorie held his hands up in surrender as Dani laughed.

"Maybe you could help Raya up Sonny and we can go back in the living room." smiled Dani.

Chapter Thirteen

Sonny was in a great mood for a Monday morning. It did not last long when he entered the station house and saw Miss Daniels sitting in the lobby.

As Sonny approached Sheryl Daniels stood and meet him half way, her eyes were bloodshot from crying. Dark circles under her eyes told him she wasn't sleeping. Something had happened to her that much was apparent. "Miss Daniels, can I help you?"

"I don't know." was the response he got between the tears. The woman was clearly shaken.

"Sheryl, come with me. Let's get you settled." Sonny scored the station for Jorie. He was the softer of the two. He would know how to comfort the hysterical woman. "Come with me there is a family room we can sit and talk privately."

Sonny caught Jorie's eye as he entered the station house. Signaling with a head nod for him to follow, Sonny guided Sheryl into the private room and helped her to a chair. Sonny heard the door close behind him as Jorie came in. "Sheryl, I need you to try and breath I need you to relax.

She nodded taking a few deep breaths, with a shaky hand she held out an envelope. As Sonny took it he started to hand it off to Jorie until Sheryl spoke. "Look in it, it's not the envelope ...but ... what's in it."

Taking back the envelope Sonny opened it and saw a pair of red glass rosary beads and a note that read *two down one to go.* "Where did you find this Miss Daniels?"

"On my front porch, when I went to get the paper this morning."

"You should have called us we would have come to you."

Shaking her head, "don't you understand I have to leave. You must let me leave. He will Just keep killing."

"Miss Daniels, is there someone we can call for you? Someone you trust that can get you, perhaps stay with?"

"Father Delacroix is the only person I really know."

"Then I will call him. I am sure he will have no problem coming."

When the water works started up again Sonny made his exit. Leaving Jorie to handle the hysterical woman. While he to the envelope with its contents down to forensics."

Jorie stepped out of the room to talk with Sonny before he called Sonny's brother. "Sonny, you think she's playing us?"

"If she is, she's good."

* * *

Could a day get any longer was the thought that crossed Sonny's mind. Waving a see ya later towards Jorie Sonny was headed home for a hot shower and a serious glass of scotch. Then things changed.

"Delacroix, you got a phone call."

"Fuck!!! "

Grabbing the phone off his desk Sonny growled a hello into the receiver. The woman on the other end was not very happy with his tone of voice and chastised him for his disrespectful behavior. Sonny's response was "yes mother." By the time, he got off the phone he was mad as hell and knew exactly who was to blame for the phone call and the visit he now had to make to his mother's home. If he found Michael between here and there he would run him over with his car.

* * *.

"Look at you, you think your smart. That was stupid, stupid, stupid. Leaving that pathetic weak woman those beads and that note. I need to be smarter, smarter than they are. She knows it's me. She told them it was me. Her time is coming. She will pay for not loving me, yes, she will.

That priest she loves so much perhaps I should kill him, no, no, no. Only the girls die, but … I could make him watch when I kill her.

* * *

Sonny thought about Dani as he drove to his mother's house. HIs plans had been to pick her up right after work and have dinner Now with this detour Sonny didn't know what time he would be able to see her. She had an interview in Baton Rouge early in the morning. If this screwed his evening up Michael would be paying the piper.

Pulling into the driveway, he could not miss his mom standing there waiting on him. He knew Michael was there by her demeanor. Damn him for sticking his nose where it did not belong. "Hey mom," Sonny called as he got out the car. "Thought you would be making dinner."

Ms. Delacroix turned on her heels and walked into the house leaving the door wide open for her son. Wiping his feet on the mat Sonny walked in the house ready for a war.

"Mom, before you start in on me about whatever it is you think I have done …his rant was short lived when he turned the corner into his mother's living room and he saw a house full of people that all yelled …SURPRISE…at the same time.

For fucks sake, he had totally forgotten it being his birthday. He had not even given it a thought. That's when he saw the two-people responsible for this little get together Raya and Dani were stuck like glue by the kitchen table.

Sonny pointed a finger at both women and signaled for them to come to him. When they looked to Jorie for help he laughed and shooed them towards Sonny. When they finally eased up to him Dani shoved Raya at Sonny first but he just reached around and pulled her into a tight hug along with Raya. "Thank you both." he whispered for only them to hear.

* * *

Dinner out with Jorie and Raya had become a weekly thing for Sonny and Dani. He was glad the two women got along so well. His mother on the other hand wanted grandchildren and now was not soon enough. Sonny had a good mind to tell her Raya was pregnant. On second thought that topic would be a shit storm. Those two better plan a quick church wedding and get things rolling along on the fast track before she started showing.

"What are you thinking about over there so hard?"

"How Raya and Jorie need to hurry up and get married."

Dani smiled then laughed as Sonny shook his head. "You laugh but, has my mother drug you into the kitchen to explain how she needs grandchildren?"

Dani laughed harder. Sonny mussed her hair as she tried catching her breath. "It's not that funny Dani, try to compose your self-woman." That only made her laugh more at his expense.

As the car pulled into the small drive to Sonny's house they noticed a light on. Dani looked at Sonny as he stopped the car. "Stay in the car Dani." Sonny grabbed a gun from the glove box chambered a round and showed Dani where the safety was. "Someone comes at you, shoot them. You hear me Dani."

"Yes." Dani didn't try to stop him as he got out of the car. She held the gun steady in her hands as she watched Sonny take to the shadows and make his way up to the house. Dani saw Sonny go into the house. When lights popped on throughout the place she knew he would be out shortly. But seconds ticked by turning to minutes. Dani was about to get out the car when Sonny came down the stairs heading straight to her.

Sonny got behind the wheel, putting the car in gear he said nothing. When he parked the car, he realized she was still holding the gun. He gently took it from her hands, placing it back in the glove box he told her to stay in the car until he came around and got her out. Dani agreed.

When her door opened, Sonny held out his hand for her to it. When she was standing in front of him he kissed her gently. "Thank you for letting me handle this alone."

"You're the cop."

"Very true. Let's go inside and discuss those boots you have on."

"You like these boots."

"No, I love those boots and the things you do while wearing them."

"Sonny, there is something I wanted to ask you."

Stopping in the garage he looked down at her and waited as she nibbled on her bottom lip while she thought things over before she spoke. Finally, she looked at him.

"You remember when I wore these last?"

"Yes, I do."

"Well, I wore these tonight to have a bargaining chip."

"Really."

"Yes, I want to use those hooks and sashes on you."

Sonny looked at her and damn his dick got hard thinking about being tied to the headboard while she rode him with those fuck me thigh high leather boots on. He didn't respond with words he just tossed her over his shoulder and made easy work of the stairs. There was a bed calling his name.

Dani laughed, as she found herself ass end up over Sonny's shoulder. It was becoming a habit for him to just toss her around like he was alpha in the relationship who was she kidding he was all alpha male.

When he placed Dani on her feet she wobbled a second before gaining her balance and then laughed when he yanked the covers from the bed and let them land on the floor in a heap.

"I take it you like my offer."

Sonny tipped her head all the way up with his index finger by placing it under her chin. "No one and I mean no one has ever been curious about being the one in control. I'm not saying I will like it but, for you I am willing to give it a go. Only if you keep the boots on."

"Oh, the boots are staying on whether I'm in control or not."

"I'll let you play." With that Dani found herself being tossed on the bed and Sonny coming at her full force. When she scrambled back from him he grabbed a leather glad foot and yanked her back towards him. "I didn't say when you could have your turn now did I."

*   *   *

Lori had made a mistake by going in Sonny's house and turning on a light. She now hid in a coat closet by the front door waiting for the fuckers to get on with their evening so she could get out.

When it sounded like they were in the bedroom she opened the door slowly and slipped out. She was at the door when she heard the moans. Being the way she was she licked her lips as she listened. She could peek. Lori loved watching Sonny fuck. She really liked when he took them hard and fast not giving them time to recover from one moment to the next. Easing her way through the house she moved into the hall where the door to the bedroom lay open.

Hugging the wall, she got all the way to the doorframe where she could see everything through the mirror and they couldn't see her. She had been watching him for years. Anytime he seemed to like one more than another she made sure to remind him of his promises. This little bitch lately had her hooks in him deep.

Lori watched ass Dani slid up and down slowly on Sonny's cock, smiling *he doesn't like slow and steady bitch.* Then Dani reached up in the headboard and pulled out the steel rings and the sashes out. *Was this bitch going to tie him up?*

* * *

Dani licked her lips at the thought of tying Sonny up and fucking him, she was already soaked from riding him slow and easy. Now tightening the sashes around his thick wrist, she was in control. She kissed and nibbled her way down to his cock and ran her tongue over it then she straddled him backwards. Dani tossed her hair over her shoulders so it cascaded down her back, her boot heels grazed Sonny's sides as she eased down on him. Sliding her hands forward she gripped his legs. What started as seduction became clawing need to have more. She was putting on a show for him. Dani hoped he liked it as her ass rose and fell slapping against his thighs. As Sonny tried to force her to move faster she did the opposite and slowed down which only ignited the fire between her legs.

Dani was trying to hold back the orgasm that threatened to take her over she just wanted Sonny to get there with her, but it was coming so fast. She felt Sonny's hand slide over her ass. *Damn he had gotten loose. Thank god, he could take over without her having to stop.* Sonny didn't stop her he didn't want to he just wanted. He slipped a finger down around the base of his cock getting it nice and wet then ran it up and around Dani's ass when he heard her moan he pressed his finger into her sweet tight ass and her body exploded around his greedy cock as she bucked against his finger and his cock. He managed to get the other hand free.

Sonny flipped her over grabbed the ties and synced her hands up tight. Pulling her body back towards him he reentered her slamming against her the sound of her crying out for him to fuck her harder had him losing all sense of control. Sonny shoved her head down onto the bed gripped her hips and continued pounding until there was only the sound of begging he didn't know who was doing the most him or her but they both couldn't get enough.

* * *

Lori stumbled back from the bedroom doorway. Stunned truly stunned Sonny had given Dani control even if it was only minutes he had given it to her. She rushed to the door the whole while hearing their moans and screams rang in her ears. Lori found herself in the garage starring at Sonny's car. Lori turned to leave as fast as possible she wanted to scream.

That's when she saw the bat. Grabbing a rag from. a box against the wall she picked up the bat, heading for Sonny's car. "Fuck you Sonny!"

Chapter Fourteen

The alarm went off way too early for Sonny's liking. As he went to reach over to shut the fucker off he realized Dani was draped across his chest. With the alarm blaring he stopped to admire the beautiful woman in his bed.

"Please if you care any for me turn off that fucking alarm!"

Sonny hit the button and rolled over taking Dani with him. "I could get use to waking up like this."

"Me too Sonny. What time is it?"

"Seven."

Dani jumped up like the house was on fire. "Shit, I'm going to be late. I have a meeting in less than two hours in Baton Rouge. Shit, fuck, hell."

Sonny laughed as he lay there watching her scramble around for all of five minutes. "Dani, stop." When she stopped, and looked at him she had to blow hair from her face to do so. "Darlin, you brought clothes over just in case you stayed the night. Go get in the shower, I will start the coffee."

Dani climbed back in bed just to kiss him. "Can I have toast also?"

"I think for toast I should get to shower with you."

"If you shower with me there won't be time for toast.

Sonny slapped Dani on the ass as she climbed from the bed. "Damn woman that's one fine ass." Sonny slipped on lounge pants and made his way to the kitchen as he did so he flipped on the news. Weather man said clear and cold again.

Dani came out of the bedroom to the smell of coffee and toast. Sonny looked up from the news just to watch her walk through the living room.

"There's a go mug on the counter for you."

"Thank you, babe."

Sonny nodded thinking that was a first.

"I made the bed. Hope that's okay?"

"That was sweet. Thanks." Seemed there were lots of first going on.

Dani dropped a kiss on his lips and told him bye. She would catch up later. Sonny finished his coffee and headed for the shower.

* * *

Sonny turned the TV off rinsed his coffee cup, grabbed his coat and keys. As he headed for the garage entrance he remembered to check the front door first. It was locked. "Good girl."

Entering the garage Sonny saw the bat sticking out of the front window of his car. "What in the fuck!" Looking at the smashed window his first instinct was to yank the fucking bat out and go postal on the rest of the car, the detective side of him kicked into high gear. Opening his phone, he called Jorie.

"Morning lover." laughed Jorie when he answered.

"I need a forensic team at my place."

"What's going on Sonny?"

"Jorie just get over here with a team. I've had a break in."

"Give me ten."

Sonny couldn't just stand there looking at his car so he went back upstairs to wait and try to calm his raging temper. Standing starring out the front window of his living room, He wondered how he had not heard anything last night. He went over his evenings events. He had gotten in around eight pm his female companion had come over at nine pm. Retracing his steps Sonny deducted that the break in had to have happened after his company had arrived.

Slipping his jacket off he hung it over a chair and sat down. If it wasn't eight am he would have a drink. Not being able to just sit there he got up and began to pace, his mood was not improving as the minutes ticked by.

When he heard Jorie come through the door he instantly jumped his ass.

"Where the fuck have you been? Your place is less than ten minutes."

"I wasn't at home Sonny. I do have a life, not that you ever ask about it."

Turning towards the garage door Sonny mumbled a sorry and kept walking down the stairs sure Jorie would follow suit. Entering the garage, he heard Jorie let out a slow whistle as he came up behind him.

Jorie shook his head, "Sonny who have you pissed off lately?"

"I have no clue. This is the fourth incident in the past month. Once forensics has gone over the garage maybe we will have a clue."

"I hope so. But as you know there hasn't been any found on the last two crime scenes involving your personal space."

Sonny looked at his car. There wasn't any other damage done to the exterior of the car that he saw. He was waiting for the forensics team to get there so he could look inside. Whoever was playing with him he would find them and whatever game they were playing he would figure it out. When he did get his hands on them it would be one introduction they would never forget. As the garage door lifted open Sonny turned towards Jorie with a questioning look.

"No need for us to go back upstairs to answer the door when we will just have to come back down."

"Maybe you want to stand out in the freezing cold but I don't."

Sonny left Jorie standing in the garage as he headed back upstairs.

Sonny hadn't kept time as he waited for Jorie to let him know the team had gotten there so when he stepped into the kitchen Sonny was surprised when Jorie said the forensics team was finished and had left. It was time for he and Jorie to go over the crime scene. Jorie asked if Sonny wanted another detective to handle the scene. Not happening was the response he got. Jorie should have known that was coming.

"Let's go work the scene."

"After you, boss."

Sonny grabbed a coat from the closet and headed downstairs. With this starting off his day it would be a long one. Jorie started in on the questioning as they headed downstairs. It would take all of his patience to deal with the questions. Questions he did not want to answer.

The first one was a normal run of the mill question always asked.

"Sir where were you last night between nine p.m. and this morning when you found the car." Jorie tried not to laugh but he just couldn't help his self.

Sonny didn't respond.

Jorie saw the tick in Sonny's jaw start. He loved getting under his skin.

"Det. Delacroix, it would help me if you could answer my questions."

"Jorie damn it! I was here and yes, I had company all night. I didn't hear anything."

"Could your company have heard anything?"

"I doubt it. I'm sure if Dani had heard anything she would have said something"

Before Jorie could ask another question, Sonny pointed a finger at him letting Jorie know to stop with the questions. He wanted to go over the interior and exterior of the car which meant underneath the car and under the hood.

It didn't take long simply because Sonny kept his car immaculate. It was so always show room ready. Jorie couldn't ever remember Sonny ever allowing a dirty foot in the car. Sonny always took his own car unless they happen to be out on a call together and then he road with Jorie in their unmarked.

"Anything?"

"Nothing underneath or under the hood."

There wasn't any sign of anyone being in the car or in the hood either. "It looks like they just smashed the window and left."

"If they got passed the security to get in the garage do you think they were in the house while . . . ummm . . . you entertained?"

The thought hadn't crossed Sonny's mind. What if someone had been in the house watching him with Dani. It should not matter what he did on his own time in the privacy of his home. But, he did not want someone using his private life against him. Thinking about someone being in his home had him reaching for his phone.

"Who are you calling now?"

"Dani. I want her back here asap. This nut job could have their sights on her as well."

"Has she said anything happening at her place?"

"No, she hasn't said anything. Damn it I should have called her as soon as I saw this. She's already in her meeting."

"Call the forensics team back. I want the doorknobs and door frames dusted for prints."

"Listen Sonny I don't think that's a good idea. I have a small finger print kit in my trunk lets you and I do the house."

Sonny had to agree with Jorie. Bringing the others back and letting them into his home could be taking a chance he wasn't willing to take. What he did in his home was his business.

Sonny tried one more time calling Dani, this time he finally got her on the phone.

"Hello."

"Dani, where are you?"

"On the freeway, why?"

"Someone broke in last night while we were home."

"OMG"

* * *

Lori followed Dani down I-10 heading from New Orleans to Baton Rouge. "Let's see where you're going you little bitch."

* * *

After a day from hell Sonny and Jorie were glad it was quitting time. Right up to the point the captain called them into his office. "Gentlemen this is FBI special agent Charlie Canon. He is here to help with the investigation."

And the night wasn't over, reaching for his phone Sonny hoped Dani answered. When she finally answered, Sonny told her he had to stay later then he had hoped. He did not want her at his place alone.

Dani was all about that. She had some studying to do for an online class she had picked up and was good with just staying home. She made him promise to call her when he got in.

Chapter Fifteen

All Dani wanted was a hot shower, a glass of wine and possible food. Traffic had been a nightmare coming out of Baton Rouge. A pile up on the I-10 had traffic at a standstill for hours. Stripping off her work clothes, making her way to the kitchen for that glass of wine before jumping in the shower.

* * *

Sonny dialed Dani's number as he got in his car. It had been an all-around v long night. He was hungry and tired but what he wanted was his woman lying next to him. Now if she would pick up the phone he would bribe her with the promise of a massage one she could give to him. Sonny smiled at the thought.

Sonny was a little disappointed when Dani didn't answer her phone. Looking at his watch he realized it was after midnight. She was probably in bed. Sonny put the phone away and headed home.

* * *

Dani lie on the floor her lip was busted she could taste blood in her mouth. One of her eyes was swollen shut. She couldn't see who the person was that attacked her when she got home. Now a lamp shined in her face keeping her from seeing anything. Whoever it was hadn't tried to rape her so far. But she was only in her bra and panties. She had been about to get into the shower when she was struck from behind. That much she did remember.

Now tied up like a Christmas turkey she just lay there waiting for Sonny to save her. Dani was counting on m to save her.

* * *

Sonny heard the buzz of his phone, he was too tired to answer the blasted thing but it just kept ringing. Rolling over he grabbed it off the night stand and growled into it.

"Sonny…."

"Dani?"

"Sonny ...can .... can you come to my place?"

"Dani, what's going on?"

He heard Dani cry out in pain. As he heard a hard slap. "Dani .... Dani......!!!! "

Her strangled plea was heard that time. "Sonny....don't come…"

Sonny heard a shot and the phone went dead. Sonny got up and dressed. Sliding his shoulder harness on he checked the sig and slipped it back into the holster. Sonny did the same with the gun at his waist and his holdout at his ankle. He wasn't taking chances someone was trying to get his attention. Dani was a sweet woman if someone was hurting her because of him it would be a beating they never forgot. Grabbing his keys and phone he called Jorie as he made his way to his car.

* * *

"Impressive job Dani. Now we wait for Sonny boy to get here and then you go away like the rest of them."

Tears flowed down Dani's face. Her side was on fire she watched as blood seeped from the wound. Dani clung to the idea it was only a flesh wound. Sonny would come he would at least get the asshole that did this to her Dani was sure of it. Sonny may not be willing to say he loved her. But, he acted like a man that did. Dani thought about that as she tried to suppress a moan.

"You can moan Dani. I know you want to. Sonny makes you moan? He used to make me moan. He liked the way I moaned. Sonny should have kept his promise and never loved anyone else"

"He doesn't love me."

"Right he just fucks you. Tell me why does Sonny let you watch as he fucks you. You should answer me Dani I don't like rude people."

The slap to her face slammed Dani's head against the floor. She thought she heard birds then she realized it was a siren. Dani prayed that her captive didn't decide she was no longer needed.

"Oh, here comes your knight in shining armor. Too bad this is just where I can kill him. But first we will see if he cares about you dear. I want you to know I will make sure he watches as you bleed to death. It's only fair for me to rip you out of his life like he was ripped out of mine."

"Why me Dani whispered."

"What was that dear? Why you? I will tell you while we wait for Sonny to get in here. Because not that you believe it Sonny loves you. I know my man and he lets you have some of the control. He has never allowed any of the others to touch him."

Dani moaned she just couldn't help herself. The pain ran from her head to her hip. She didn't want to hear about the other women Sonny slept with Dani knew he had others. But, it had seemed Sonny had been spending more time with her. What a fool she was.

* * *

Sonny swept the area as he made his way
from his car to the entrance to the building.
Pushing the door open he peered inside
making sure he could enter without notice.
Staying low along the staircase Sonny made
it to the second floor as he checked the
landing he proceeded up the next flight of
stairs. Dani lived on the third floor.

Her loft apartment was the third-floor Sonny
knew this because Dani told him the first
time they met. Sonny almost smiled
remembering that meeting. Dani had been
nervous and rambled on about things he
didn't care about back then. Now he wished
for once he knew the layout of an apartment.
The door was ajar so Sonny eased up to
listen.

"Sonny," Dani's assailant called out in a
gravel voice. "Won't you come in and join
us."

Sonny stepped in keeping to the shadows.
"Dani your gonna be fine I promise."

"Dani don't listen to him." Her captive smiled." Sonny has a problem promising women things and not keeping them."

"How do you know anything about me?" Sonny asked.

"Oh, Sonny I can tell you so many things about you."

Sonny stepped fully into the room gun pointed at the mysterious figure standing beyond the light... Trying to get a better look at Dani who appeared to be alive on the floor. A small puddle of blood had begun to dry at her side. Dani's hands were tied behind her back feet bound at the ankles. A lamp was pointed at her keeping Dani from being able to see her attacker.

The attacker pulled their mask off and the voice changer along with it. Sonny recognized the woman from an earlier accident he and Jorie handled close to his house." Lori Hammonds?" Sonny stated.

"Well at least you remembered my name or is that my name SONNY?"

Sonny moved a little closer to Dani, if she was alive he would get her out of here. Why had he spent so much time with her? This is what always happened Sonny let himself to get close and then they get hurt. Taking a deep breath Sonny centered himself and took aim.

"You let me check on Dani and . . ."

"And what Sonny, are you going to whisk Dani away and make things all better?"

"I want to know she' s okay."

Sonny watched as the suspect Lori Hammonds moved into the light stepping up beside Dani's body. A gun in her left hand was pointed at Dani's head. Sonny brought the gun up at Lori's chest taking aim he could remove the threat from Dani easily.

"I don't think you want to do that Sonny. I have a twitchy trigger finger. "

Lori pushed Dani's body over with her foot so Sonny could get a better look at the damage she had done to the woman. Watching his facial expression go from concern to anger riled Lori's temper. Lori reared back with her boot clad foot and kicked the unconscious Dani.

"Kick her again and I will fucking shot you in that fucking foot."

"Why not shoot me in the head Sonny?"

"Because bitch. I want you to suffer."

"What a charmer you are. I have suffered you bastard. You have no idea how I suffered."

Sonny needed to get Lori's attention off Dani. If he could get her full attention off Dani Sonny would have a clear shot. He wouldn't take a chance on Dani being injured any further. Sonny noted the slight rise and fall of Dani's chest. It was shallow but still it was something. What was it about Lori that nagged at him. Something about her that pulled at him. Had since he and Jorie worked an accident involving her weeks back. Sonny needed to get her talking.

"Why don't you tell me Lori. How have you suffered?"

"You Sonny have been so preoccupied with the serial killer case that you weren't vigilant with who was preoccupied with you."

"I suppose that, was you?"

Sonny stepped closer into the room. But it didn't help the situation. Lori stepped across Dani's body straddling her. Aiming the gun down at Dani's stomach. She wasn't going to make this easy for him.

Laughing at Sonny Lori nodded yes at him. Pushing the toe of her boot into Dani's side wound made Dani cry out. Lori sneered at Sonny when she saw the level of concern that appeared on his face.

"Isn't that sweet, you care about her. Told you Dani. She didn't believe me Sonny. Dani said you didn't love her. I told her you did. Would you like to know how I know that.?"

"Sure, tell me Lori."

Trying to look more relaxed Sonny began taking note of the best way to take down Lori and keep Dani from being harmed further. Fucking bitch had no idea who she was dealing with or what his feelings for Dani were.

"I said tell me."

"I told you I have been watching you. I left you the note. I tried to warn you Sonny. I have kept my eyes on you for years. I have watched you since the so-called love of your life died. What was her name? Jess, wasn't it?"

Dani lay as still as she possibly could, hoping the woman standing over her body would lose interest and move away from her. When She mentioned knowing the one-woman Sonny had ever loved had Dani trying to focus a little more. She knew Sonny had suffered a loss that Dani felt he had never recovered from. Would this deranged woman holding her captive at gun point tell the story?

"I watch you with those women. I have followed you to the tomb Jess's tomb. I have herd your words, your lies."

Pissing him off was not going to go well for Lori. Sonny had known he had been followed but could never prove it. This had to be the person who broke into his home and smashed his wind shield and broke things in his home.

"How have I lied? If you know me so well, tell me."

"You tell her that you have kept your promise. That she still the only one that you love. You tell her there will never be another. Tell me Sonny isn't that a lie now?"

"I have always loved Jess and will always love her."

"Lies, all lies !!!!!"

"I'm not lying about my feelings for Jess!"

Why was he arguing with this nut job? He needed to get to Dani. Taking another step closer forced Lori to watch him. As he stepped to the right she turned slightly to her left keeping him in her sight.

"Sonny you aren't helping Dani. You're actually killing her every step you take and you are lying. You missed spending your birthday with her. You spent it with Dani."

He had made the decision not to go that evening to the cemetery he chose to go the next day. This bitch had broken into his home and been following him.

"I went the next day. Jess would want me happy."

"That wasn't your tradition, was it? You and Jess always spent birthday's together. So, you broke your promise hence you lied."

Fuck this Sonny was done talking he heard Jorie moving closer to the door. This bitch was going down. Just when he thought he had the upper hand Lori surprised him.

"Jorie don't be shy, do come in darling." called Lori.

Sonny looked at her taken back. That one word sent chills down his spine. It was the way she said it. It couldn't be. Sonny looked at Lori with the light from the lamp hitting her at the angle throwing shadows across her face. Then he saw it. Her smile as she realized she had given herself away. Dropping the act Lori changed her whole demeanor. As her facial features softened and she relaxed her stature Sonny saw glimpses of who she really was.

"Jess?"

"Sonny."

"You can't be Jess. She died."

"No, I lived."

"Why Jess? Where, how?" Sonny would play into Lori's delusion until he got her subdued.

"I have been to heaven and hell and everywhere in between." As Lori spoke she stepped back from Dani's body and took a step towards Sonny. That's when everything went sideways. Dani moaned Sonny's name as Jorie stepped in the room gun drawn. Lori swung around bringing her gun up and

Sonny heard the click of the hammer. In a split second, he had fired at the same time as both Jorie and Lori did. Sonny heard a grunt come from Jorie as Lori fell to the ground over Dani's body. Before he could take a step, another shot rang out and then everything went quiet.

Moving quickly Sonny rolled Lori off Dani finding Lori had fired another round into herself. Whether it was on purpose or not they would never know, she was dead.

Sonny felt for a pulse on Dani finding her still alive he called out to Jorie to call it in. He looked up as at Jorie making sure he was okay. Jorie was holding inspecting his upper arm as he made the call.

Sonny untied Dani's ankles and moved her just enough to untie her hands so he could lay her down more comfortably. Grabbing a blanket from her sofa he covered her. Lori must have caught her either about to get dressed or undressed. Because Dani was in only her bra and panties.

Jorie stepped over crouching down to look at Lori.

"Isn't this the woman involved in that accident weeks back?"

"Yes, and my stalker. She admitted following me. She said she was the one that was in my house, did the damage to the car and left that note back before thanksgiving."

"What the hell Sonny."

"Jorie she knew about Jess and somehow thought she was her."

Jorie looked at Sonny with sympathy. This day was not gonna get any easier before they found out all of the story. Jorie told Sonny he had a bad feeling that something was coming. One day Sonny would listen to him.

Chapter Sixteen

It seemed like hours had passed to Sonny by the time the ambulance and other officers arrived on the scene. He was reluctant to let go of Dani's hand as the paramedics arrived to tend to her and take her to the hospital.

As he watched the ambulance drive off he was left to deal with the shooting. The police chief and superintended where now on sight. It was procedure for them to come to a shooting that involved an officer. Sonny knew the drill this was not is first rodeo.

Approaching a somber looking Jorie Sonny got a sinking feeling there was something terribly wrong.

"What is it?" He asked his Chief.

Jorie shrugged at their chief and looked at the ground. When he looked up at Sonny there was a sheen of tears in his eyes. Sonny turned back around towards the direction that the ambulance was heading. The sirens were still going so it wasn't Dani. Looking back at Jorie and their Chief. He asked what.

What happened next would change everything for Sonny. The chief handed over an I.D. that was found in a bag that had been stashed in the stairwell. Sonny took the I.D. in his hand. Before he turned it over he looked at Jorie once more. And as tears spilt from Jorie's eyes Sonny thought he would throw up. Jorie turned away trying to compose his self as Sonny turned the I.D. over and saw the picture of Lori Hammonds the name said something different. Sonny blinked a couple times trying to see clear.

It couldn't be so. The name read Jessica Batiste. Sonny just stared at the woman's picture. She didn't look anything like the Jessica Batiste he knew that they knew. Sonny looked at Jorie and shook his head no. Jorie walked back to him and put his forehead against Sonny's something they use to do when they were younger as he did so he held the back of Sonny's head in his hand holding him in place. Closest thing to a hug Sonny would give.

"Jorie, Sonny we need your weapons."

Taking a deep breath Jorie stepped back removed his weapon from its holster, disarming it and handing it over to the forensics team. Sonny followed in doing the same.

Sonny didn't remember who drove him to the station. His mind was somewhere else trying to put the pieces together. So many questions he needed answers for. He now sat in interrogation waiting for I.A. to come talk to him about the shooting. Sonny thought about Jorie he had been clipped by a bullet. Sonny also was worried about Dani's condition.

As he thought about Dani the door opened and a young detective walked in looking overly confident. Sonny smiled at the two-way mirror. Who were they kidding sending this kid in here to question him. It was a joke.

"*Detective Delacroix you need to take a seat so we can clear this matter up.*"

Sonny placed his suit jacket over the back of the empty chair and took a seat. His gun had been taken in to evidence. When a police officer was involved in a shooting it was regulations to have their sidearm taken Sonny told himself this more than once over the course of his career.

"Detective can you tell me what was the relationship between you and the victim was?"

Sonny looked at the young Detective across the table. "We were in a relationship?" Sonny questioned back.

"Can you elaborate on that. Please."

Sonny gave the younger detective a drool stare. Sliding his hand across the table Sonny asked him. "First, which victim are we discussing?"

Sonny didn't reply. He just waited for an answer.

"The deceased one. Now can you tell me how long you knew the victim? How long you had been in the so-called relationship?"

"How long have you been a detective? A year." Sonny questioned back.

"Six months."

Sonny just eased back in his chair. He wasn't about to start a pissing match with the guy.

"Again Mr. Delacroix, how long?'

"We met over a month ago, on a case. But the relationship has been going on for half my life. And it's Detective Delacroix." Sonny did not need this. He needed to be at the hospital with Dani. He had sent Raya there when Jorie refused to go until the Sonny was able to. He desperately wanted an update.

"I don't understand. Either it's you met a month ago or …. what thirty years ago?"

Looking at the younger detective Sonny replied. "It would be twenty."

"What case?"

"A car accident, and before you ask we were running down a suspect in a homicide case when the accident happened it we were first on scene. Not that I have to explain anything to you."

"How was she involved in the case?"

"She wasn't involved in the case, she was in one of the cars."

The door to the interrogation room swung open and Sonny smiled as two FBI agents walked in. Roddy who had once been on the force flipped through a folder as he spoke he never even looked at the Detective trying to get information from Sonny.

"Detective Johnson you can go we have this."

Johnson got up scooping up his notebook and stormed out glaring at Sonny the whole way.

"Sonny how we doing?"

"As well as can be expected."

"Okay let's go over this crap situation and get you out of here."

"Sounds good." Sonny knew he would be riding a desk till the investigation was concluded. He knew it was a clean shoot. How the others would find it was as good as anyone s guess. He was still reeling from the whole thing. How could Jess have been alive all these years and none of them know.

"Let's start at the beginning."

Sonny turned toward the window thinking about a month ago. . ..

* * *

Walking out of the interrogation room Sonny couldn't believe who was standing talking to Jorie.

"Francis?"

The man talking to Jorie looked at Sonny and stared him down.

"It's been a long-time Rene."

"What are you doing here?"

Francis looked at Jorie then to Sonny. Shaking his head. "I knew I should have called you a long time ago Rene.

Sonny hated when his family used his formal name, it always meant something bad was coming right behind.

"I'm on my way to identify my wife's body and make arrangements for her to be brought to the funeral home.

"Francis I am very sorry for your loss. How did she die?"

Francis's looked at his brother and knew this was probably going to go bad in so many ways.

"You shot and killed her."

It took a minute to realize what his brother said. Before Sonny even thought about what he was about to do he reacted like a man possessed.

Blind rage weld up in Sonny. Without thinking he lunged forward striking Francis across the face. He had never hated one of his brothers but he seethed hatred for Francis right then. How the hell had he not known Francis and Jess had a thing.

Before he could get another hit in Jorie pushed him back. While Francis's boys stepped in front of him.

"What's going on out here?" Called the captain.

"It's a family squabble captain that's all. Right boys?"

"You're not taking her!!!!! "Sonny gritted out between clinched teeth.

"You can't stop me Rene she's my wife."

"How long were you seeing each other behind my back Francis? I deserve to know."

"If you have to ask me that you never knew Jess."

Sonny didn't get to ask any other questions Francis walked away with his goons.

Shoving Jorie from him he looked squarely at his captain. He knew what he looked like, this was the man he kept leashed the man he held tight someone he didn't like very much.

"I'm not riding the desk till this shit is over. I will take suspension with or without pay."

"Sonny just use some personal time off, lord knows you have enough saved up."

Reaching for his gun and badge sonny realized his gun was evidence in the investigation. He looked at Jorie but refrained from saying anything else. Sonny just needed to get out of there. As sonny exited the building he ran into his brother.

Sonny turned to walk in the opposite direction.

"Don't turn away like a fucking coward Rene."

"What did you just call me sonny called out as he spun around. You know better than anyone I'm not a fucking coward."

"There are things you don't know and I won't discuss them on the streets. When you're ready you come see me and I will gladly answer them. Jess will be buried in her family's crypt."

Shaking his head sonny asked. "Who's in there now pretending to be Jess?"

"No one. We kept her funeral small. We had a closed casket so I had it weighted down."

"Why did you come to the station? You know the morgue is on Tulane now."

"I wanted to talk to you that's when I found out you killed her. Like I said when you want answers come see me."

"I can find my own answers brother !!!!" With that sonny turned and walked away from Francis. Where he was headed, he didn't know. For years, he talked to Jess when things threatened to fall apart. Stopping in his tracks he turned back he needed to do just that. He needed to talk to Jess because his heart was completely shattered beyond what he had thought it could ever be again.

Sonny slid into his car and just sat there. Leaning over the steering wheel he closed his eyes. All he could see was Jess pointing the gun at Jorie and pulling the trigger he had acted so fast he didn't have time to even think he just reacted when she spun around and shot at him. Jorie had dropped to the ground managing to only get hit in the arm. Sonny hadn't known it was even Jess, she looked so different. Blinking back tears he refused to let fall Sonny started the car and Headed straight to the morgue.

Sonny stopped outside the door, taking a deep breath he centered himself. Pushing open the door he saw the medical examiners assistant.

"May I help you detective?"

"I need to see Jessica Delacroix's body."

"Yes sir, she's over here. Would you like a few minutes before we let the funeral home take her?"

"Yes, thank you."

Following the assistant, he stood as he folded back the sheet. Sonny watched as the young man walked away leaving him alone.

"All these years Jess all this is time. Couldn't you have come to me told me the truth. What did I do to make you leave me? To hate me so that I had to suffer for a life that now I find out wasn't over. Now I find out all this time you were happily married to Francis."

"I wouldn't say she was happily married."

Sonny looked over his shoulder at his brother Michael.

"Please don't tell me you knew. Oh, god you knew and let me go through my life blaming myself for her death. Why Michael tell me why. For the love of god why!"

"I have only known for a brief time. I tried to find a way to tell you without breaking my vows. I took her confession and you know my hands were tied. She laughed when she told me said she liked seeing me miserable, that she would have you twisting in the wind as well."

"What does that mean?"

"I don't know?" Sonny's brother replied.

"Rene ......"

Sonny closed his eyes Michael never used his formal name. The name was a sore spot with him. They only used it when they wanted him focused on what they had to say. Turning to give his brother his full attention he waited.

"I think you should go talk to Francis. There's more to all this then we know."

"You mean then I know right FATHER."

"You should talk to him."

"I don't want to talk to him. If you don't mind I would like some time with Jess before they take her away."

Michael went to put his hand on Sonny's shoulder and stopped himself. His brother didn't want his brother nor his priest right now. He did what Sonny asks and left him to be alone with the one woman he loved his whole life. Michael wished he could tell him everything Jess had told him. If Sonny would just talk to Francis he would have the answers he so desperately needed. One more glance back at Sonny Michael left him there with his head hung, his hands white knuckled on the table.

Epilogue

three days later:

Sonny had taken a break from sitting at the hospital to meet Jorie to talk. He just wanted a minute to process things. He had not left Dani's side over the past three days. She was in and out of consciousness because of the pain killers they had her on. Sonny couldn't bring himself to leave her to wake and him not be there. Raya had come to sit with her while he went to meet Jorie.

He still wanted to kill Francis. Simply for the lies. Sonny realized sitting in that cold hospital room watching Dani recover that he and Jess would have never lasted. How had he been so convinced that everything that happened to her was his fault.

"Sonny, I know that look and none of this is your fault." Jorie spoke from behind

Sonny. He knew his brother well enough to know what he was thinking.

Opening the door to the bar both men stepped in not saying another word. Until they sat down.

"Jorie did you know she was alive? Did you know it was her?"

"Sonny, none of us recognized Jess. We all thought she was dead. Come on did you have any clue it was her?"

When Sonny glared at him Jorie sighed. "I had to ask."

Sonny looked down at the scotch in his glass.

"Did you ask her why? Or how she survived? I mean shit… I was a fucking pall bearer at her fucking funeral for Christ sakes."

"I ask her those exact questions while I was trying to reason with her. She said she had been to heaven, hell and everywhere in between."

"Do you think she killed those women?"

"She didn't say that. She said I chose other women over her."

"Had you been cheating on Jess?"

"NO! Jorie I was not."

"Okay."

"Then why did she say you chose other women over you?"

"Because I didn't stay true to her over the years. That is the only thing I can figure."

Looking up at himself in the mirror behind the bar Sonny noticed for the first time how tired he looked. Hell he even looked old. Hell he felt old. He needed a break.

"What are we thinking over there?"

"That I need some time off . . .".

Sonny stood up starred at Jorie and turned walking away. Jorie watched as the one man he considered his brother walk away. He knew Sonny was hurting and probably a lot confused at that moment. The one person he had felt he let down had been the determining factor of his life and right about now Sonny was probably second guessing every single one. . .

"Excuse me, were you guy's talking about the rosary murders?"

Jorie looked over at a guy sitting at the end of the bar. "The what murders?" asked Jorie.

"The rosary murders." Replied the guy.

"Not sure what you're talking about?"

"That's what the locals are calling those murders. The ones that the cops found with rosary beads in their hands."

As the guy explained he eased past Jorie heading out the door. Jorie turned to respond but the guy disappeared through the crowd coming in to the bar. Jorie realized a second to late that the guy had said the beads had been in the victim's hands. That was not the case, they had been wrapped around their necks in the two murders in the city. The murders on the east coast from years ago those victims held the beads in their hands.

Pushing through the crowd Jorie finally made it out on to the street. Looking up and down he couldn't find the guy anywhere. Grabbing his phone Jorie went to dial sonny then decided to call the precinct he needed to get with a sketch artist now.

*   *   *

Stupid, stupid!! You should have stayed away from the cops.

Want to know more about the author:

You can follow her on Facebook at Author Roux Cantrell

And on Instagram

Between control,

and chaos is where the devil plays.

Roux

Made in the USA
Columbia, SC
03 May 2017

70265057R00142 ·

Made in the USA
Columbia, SC
03 May 2017